BICHU THE JAGUAR

D1613153

No sound. The bullet's whine is lost in the jungle's living hum. Bichu feels nothing as the missile plunges through her body. Then shock, pain, fear stun her. Instinct drives her to her feet. She must battle to live, to get across the South American pampas to her mountain home.

A jungle Indian with his young daughter reads the message Bichu's tracks leave in the soft sand. 'An *onca*, a jaguar. It is a small one, a female, and she walks on three legs, and there is blood, she has been hurt.' The hunt is on.

Bichu
The Jaguar

Alan Caillou

Illustrations by Alex Tsao

CORONET BOOKS
Hodder Paperbacks Ltd., London

Copyright © 1969 by Alan Caillou
Illustrations Copyright © 1969
First printed in Great Britain for
Hodder & Stoughton Ltd, 1971
Coronet edition 1971

Printed and bound in Great Britain for
Coronet Books, Hodder Paperbacks Ltd,
St. Paul's House, Warwick Lane,
London, E.C.4
By Hunt Barnard Printing Ltd,
Aylesbury, Bucks.

ISBN 0 340 15117 X

chapter one

Bichu was wounded, and she was going home to die.

She was hurt badly. The bullet that was deep inside her long, smooth body had smashed through her soft, resilient skin just forward of her right shoulder; it had glanced aside from the collarbone, and continued, twisting over and over, through the muscles under the right flank; it had turned on a rib, which it had split, and then passed on, almost spent now, to come to rest against the wall of her stomach.

Her first reaction had been an instinct, no more. She had streaked for half-glimpsed cover, heading for the deep shadows, falling unexpectedly when the rush of acute pain hit her, and then struggling to her feet again and moving like yellow lightning into the spotted shade of the forest.

And there she lay, in shock, not understanding what had happened nor why, panting and trying to turn her head far enough to lick the blood that was pulsing out of the wound. For a moment the bright eyes glazed over, dulling, and then she rolled over onto her back and pawed at the air, trying to force it into her lungs, as though the pain were nothing and the only thing to fear was the inability to breathe. For nearly a minute the pain was almost forgotten in her desperate search for oxygen, and then it came flooding over her, bursting, throbbing, blinding her, clouding her eyes. She almost seemed to know that she was dying.

There was blood welling up in her throat, and the need to cough was almost insuperable. And but for one thing, she would have lain there, the battle over, waiting till death swept over her and left her beautiful body to become part of the forest humus that fertilized the trees and the bushes and the vines, making their life stronger with her death.

The thing that brought her, with shocking suddenness, back to her senses was the second shot. She heard the bullet add its sharp clip to the singing of the forest all around her. And to her quick ear the second shot had been a trifle closer; not much, not much more than a few yards, but the infinitesimal difference was there. It was still a long way off, but she braced herself for more of the pain, and when it did not come, when there was only silence again, the old instincts took over, and she moved, slowly now and with infinite caution, close to the ground, dragging her belly over the moss, moving in silence, because silence was necessary now, as it sometimes was in times of acute danger. She turned aside for every dried twig that might snap, for every cluster of dried leaves that might rustle. Bichu had been hunted before, and evasion was a tactic she knew well, had learned well from her mother on that long chase that had ended, not many years ago, with the death of both her parents.

She had been a cub then, scarcely weaned. And she had lain under a bush that was hardly big enough to provide cover for a mouse, hiding herself as her mother had taught her, and watching while the callous hunters dragged the two yellow bodies, spotted with dapple brown, over to the trees. They strung them up by the feet from low branches and expertly stripped off the skins. There had been dogs, and the hunters had thrown them the bloody carcasses, and the dogs had torn at them savagely, gorging themselves. She had lain there watching all day, feeling the scent of the blood on the sharp wind that came to her from them, her eyes alert and seeking further cover should the wind change and take her scent to the dogs. When they had all gone with their dogs, she had waited a long time before creeping over to settle down beside all that was left of them, bewildered because the friendly, lively smells were no longer there. She could not understand just why she was now alone.

All through the evening she had stayed there, waiting for some kind of a miracle which would show her that this bloodied mess was not really the flesh of her parents. There were green eyes all around her, and she could smell the jackals, and when, cautiously, two of them approached the meat, she slashed out with her needle-sharp claws, gashing open a cruel muzzle, and drove them away. The flapping in the trees above her had told her of vultures, and when they began to drop down and settle restlessly near the meat, she had streaked in among them, young and immature as she was, using her claws and her teeth until they took to the trees again.

A coati, ring-tailed, long-nosed, and inquisitive, fully grown and dangerous, crept close to her and watched her for a while, gauging her age and her competence. It was a friendly sort of creature, but its temper was unpredictable, and sometimes it would attack, for no apparent reason, anything that invaded its territory. It made a sudden dash at her; she leaped aside to avoid the clutching paws that could rip her back wide open, and struck out at the long snout, cutting it and gouging out an eye; and when the coati, squealing, slipped back into the bushes, Bichu had come to realize that she had no one to protect her; her destiny, now, was hers alone.

She thought, then, of the muscles in her shoulders, of the tight tendons along her smooth legs, of the soft padding of delicate feet on the forest floor. She knew that the forest was hers.

That was a long time ago, and now the hunters were abroad again. Listening, she lay still, not moving a muscle, frozen, forcing panic behind her till she could decipher the story of the second shot.

The sounds of the forest were many; there was the rustle of the wind through the trees, which she heard only when she began to separate it from the other sounds; there was the constant cry of the *borbetta,* the bright red parrot that so foolishly advertised its presence with too much noise; there was the very distant sound of water somewhere, a small stream, splashing over cool rocks (and this river sound registered quickly as part of an escape route); there were monkeys calling to each other, chattering stupidly because the shots had frightened them too; another bird, a toucan, was cackling; there was a plop where a snake fell from a branch and startled her; the fluttering sound of wings as a flight of patridges rose somewhere far away. She turned her head very slowly in the direction of the birds. Her eyes were wide and alert and motionless, all cloudiness gone now, though the pain was still tearing at her intestines.

And soon, from where the birds had been, she heard the sound she was waiting for. It was the sound of a human voice.

Bichu waited, crouched; her ears were alert, catching each

voiced sibilant that went on and on through the forest in a gentle wave of sound that was too low and too soft for human ears; she picked the insistence of it out of the constant sounds of the leaves and the water and the insects, knowing precisely where it came from, how far away it was, and that it spelled danger.

There were two pressing needs on her now. The old law said: *First find the danger and evaluate it.* This was the law that kept jaguars alive when everything around them conpired to kill them, to kill them because they were beautiful. The second law was older still. It said: *If you must lie down and let death come, then first go home, and then the earth you become part of will not be alien earth.* This was one of the laws of territory, which made each animal in the forest belong to a specific part of it.

She had strayed a long, long way from her part of the forest. For more than fourteen days she had moved south with the sun, driven abroad by an insatiable urge to find out what lay beyond the next mountain, and the next, and the one after that as well, moving fast and lithely, the young muscles rippling. Over the high hills and deep in the darkest valleys, across the rivers and fast (very fast here) across the pampas, a constant flow of rhythmic, easy motion, quick but unhurried, with always a great reserve of strength should it be needed. She did not know how or why she had come so far; she only knew that she was a long way from home and that to return now, to die, was an obsession.

Here were alien trees in an unfriendly forest.

Somewhere, a long way from here, there was a great green banana tree that had fallen in the rains last winter across a dark-purple slash in a sandstone slope that was the cave where she had been born; from the cave she could look out over a vast panorama of treetops, dark green and light green, moss green and emerald green, touched here and there with red and purple and yellow patches of ebullient flowers that had grown on their vines high into the tops of the tallest trees, reaching always for the sun. There was a stream nearby where sometimes she would lie on the bank with one paw in the water, waiting for an unwary fish (keeping a sharp eye out for the savage piranhas, which, she knew, would rip her foreleg to pieces if she were not quick enough). There was a shaded trail where the scents were clean and friendly and where sometimes a pheasant would strut into her waiting ambush; it was pleasing to think now of the foolish pheasants, strutting so frequently into the long grass, where, almost by habit, she would wait for them; it was as though they did not know that their territory had been invaded by a hungry intruder that would not recognize their claim to it. There was a long, narrow patch of yellow moss where she would sometimes roll to clean the soft fur of her belly. There was a deep pool where once, many years ago, she had seen some otters playing; one of them was bigger than she was, nearly seven feet long from snout to tail.

And there, above all, was safety, safety in the precise knowledge she had of the ground, in the wind which funneled along the bluff where the cave was and brought her the scents of danger long before the danger itself. It was her home, and this was where she wanted to die.

But first, she knew, there was something that must be done.

She waited for a long time, and then, at last, the voice came again, so low that she thought she might have been mistaken. She froze. Her head did not move, but her eyes looked up and found a yellow rock, a rock of her own coloring, and for a long while she examined the shadows there, minutely, carefully, methodically. Close by there was a fallen branch, black and humid underneath, and room to squeeze through and not show herself in the sunlight.

She moved fast, in three quick bounds, and the pain pounded at her intolerably, and she heard herself whimper; but she was under the rotting branch in the shadows, trembling, feeling the wet mold on her skin, knowing the smell of a snake that was close by somewhere, a snake that would neither harm her nor provide her with food and that therefore could be ignored as she wrinkled her nose and sniffed out the other scents one by one. The breeze, so faint here as to be almost unfelt, touched the moistness of her mouth, and she turned her head in the direction where the moistness was coldest, searching out the downwind and testing it. A brief pause, another sharp look; once more a lithe and furtive movement; she was flattened close to the ground now, listening. . . .

The gray rocks again, her eyes sweeping over them; the overhanging boulders casting dark shadows on the red sand . . .the broad leaves of a banana clump hanging brokenly— ah, but not *her* trees!— and the delicate tracery of a waving fern. There was a new scent here, the meat scent of a small antelope. She could not see it, but the smell of it brought her comfort.

The rocks were too far away, and a broad red patch of sand, unshadowed, lay between her and the shelter they offered; she waited a long time, gauging its breadth, its brightness, and the darkness her own shadow would make across it. She turned her head and looked behind her into the green shrubbery, and looked back at the red sand and decided that she should not take the risk; if the pain should double her up again out there in the open . . . She became aware that without the skills she had so long accepted as part of her the jungle in which she was so much at home would become her enemy. Her speed and her agility were gone; and without them, there was nothing to rely on but her animal tenacity.

She edged back under the bushes and crept to one side, each soft paw feeling out with a touch of the utmost delicacy before any weight was put on it; the fur of her chest brushed gently across the ground as she moved with care, keeping to the shadows, keeping the damp foliage tight across her back and the glint in the sun always in one corner of her eye, pausing after every crouched move forward.

The forest is never a silent place. The legend of the silent animal is a myth in normal times. The lizard moves, and dried-up pieces of leaf break the silence. A heavy cat walks, and the twigs rustle. The antelope munches the foliage noisily, tearing at it. The tapir scurries through the brush, an alligator slurps through the mud, the monkeys leap and chatter in the treetops. The jungle is a living thing: it sighs, and moans, and chatters, and cries out; and sometimes it roars with pain. But now the whole forest seemed to fall silent to watch a dying jaguar creeping from cover to cover to find out what had caused its agony; that first, and then—home, to die.

And now, in that silence, the sound of the voice came again. It was a shade, an infinitesimal shade, louder. Was it closer? Or merely less constrained? She decided it had not moved, that it was still there, a few points to one side of the breeze on her right flank.

Another open space to cross, but greener here, with patches of yellow sand. Good. She streaked across it, and then suddenly, with the burst of energy, there came too the bitter, frightening pain in her insides, as though they were being racked with a sharp and twisted stick; she fought hard to stifle the coughing and she choked, spitting dark blood onto the sand, dropping her head and falling over and over, doubled up in pain and carried forward with her own momentum.

For a moment all consciousness went from her, and she woke again in terror to find herself lying on her side, curled up and exposed in the open with not even a branch to hide under. She streaked instinctively for the shadows, biting clear through her tongue when the pain hit her again, but knowing that out here, in the sunlight, with the voice so near, she must not stay.

Her vision was blurred now, and she fought for clarity with a wild and savage determination, forcing her senses to sharpness. Her right foreleg was dragging, and the shoulder would not support her weight, and she tumbled down a steep bank into water, fast-flowing water that was cold and clear, and she struggled to right herself.

And then she lay down and waited, panting, closing her eyes and wishing, for a moment, that death would come and take the pain away from her. And when she opened her eyes again she saw that the water was red with her blood, and the sight of it sent her scrambling up the steep bank among the ferns. The blood in her mouth was welling up, and she tried to swallow it and could not; and then she coughed, just once, loudly, knowing that there was great danger in the sound but knowing, too, that if she did not she would choke to death now, before she could fulfill either of those tasks which seemed so desperately necessary to her.

For a long time after the cough she waited, frightened and trembling at her own rashness; but all that happened was a flurry of sound behind her as the antelope, hearing her, darted deeper into the shadows, as scared as she was; the scent of it went with it, and then there was silence again.

The great trunk of a fallen tree lay across her path, black

with age, alive with fungus and a million crawling white insects; there was a chink of sunlight showing underneath it. She wormed her way forward, confident that an antelope's safety was her safety too. There were the rocks again, the granite shadow closer now, a gray wall of granite, slit here and there with patches of dark that were crevices, and slashes of bright green that were strands of lichen tumbling down from it.

For a very long time she watched the rocks, and at last she saw what she was looking for—a sign of animal life that meant there was no danger there; a lizard lay sunning itself, unafraid, its mouth open and its tail curled along the warmth of the stone. It meant safety to her; when she streaked across to the rock, the lizard had gone; she knew that somewhere close by, in the shadows of its hole, it was watching her carefully, ready to move again.

She was under the rock, fast, burrowing flat to the warm sand that seemed to wrap itself around her. For a moment she worried about the dust, but her quick eyes showed her that it had not risen high enough to be a danger; she worried about it nonetheless. She waited till she was sure that all was as it should be and then slipped quickly into the shadow of the banana clump that towered high into the hot sky, and into the shade of a great red plant that burst into brilliance against the greens and browns and yellows of the trees. The top of the rock was high above her now; her heavy, rounded head tilted back (the blood was dripping onto her chest), and she looked up; she bit hard into her bloodied tongue, tensed, and leaped in two quick bounds up to the top.

She was ready for the pain; it swept over her like an avalanche, almost driving the consciousness away, and her eyes began to glaze. She shook her head to clear them, and now. . . . Now she was where she wanted to be.

This was the place. From here she could look down on the whole of the immense valley from which, in some tiny pinpoint among the greenery, the sound of the voice had come; this, for the moment, was all she wanted, to see where it had come from, to find out what was there, to explore the danger; having done this, she could let the rest take care of itself.

And there, far upwind, exactly where she had mentally placed the sound of the shots, a thin spiral of blue smoke was wisping up from a small fire, faint and indefinite; it was ethereal against the bright and constant greenery.

And the danger, she knew, was precisely there.

The voice was a whisper, hardly more than a zephyr. But there was a sibilant in the words that was carried on the breeze long after the sound of the vowels had faded, taking its time to get there, but going on and on through the forest, softer than the sound of the leaves but reaching the waiting ears (pricked up to listen for it) just the same.

The young man said softly, excitedly, "See that grass there? The bushes to the side? The moss? Somewhere in that bush, that's where he'll be."

The other man looked back over his shoulder and grunted. He said carelessly, "It was a lousy shot, you missed him, and we don't have the time to go chasing a lot of lousy cats anyway." He turned back to his work, not deigning to bother any more about it.

The hunter insisted, "I shot him. I know I did."

"Then you better get up there after him. You know how to skin a jaguar?" Grinning, he held out the long hunting knife, and the young man looked at it sourly and tossed his rifle carelessly down on the ground where the tools were laid out on a patch of rag. "All right," he said. "So I missed." He could sense the contempt, and it annoyed him. He said angrily, "Are we going to be here all day?"

"No." The older man's voice was calm. "Just a few minutes more and I'll have this thing back in the water."

They had come up from the trappers' village, the village on stilts by the edge of the river where the wild and savage mestizos lived; and they were killing time.

That's all it was, really, a way to fill in the hours till the launch should be ready to sail with its load of crocodile skins, back down the tortuous river for day after day after day, chugging along the great green river that seemed, in its haste, to tear at the trees and the ferns that lined its banks. They had borrowed the trader's decrepit outboard motor for a trip upstream to get away from the stench of the village while they waited.

Their very presence in this remote stretch of unknown land was by nothing but the most casual chance; they had come, unthinking, and soon, without having consciously learned or enjoyed or grown better by their coming, they would go.

This was the historic tragedy of this land: the white man had always come with his guns to kill; and when other things had taken his attention, he had gone again; and he had always quite forgotten that behind him there would always be a memory of his passing.

The older man was tugging at the starter rope, his legs ankle-deep in the wet mud, and the young hunter sat glumly staring at him, knowing the motor would never start, knowing they should have stayed in the café and gotten drunk on the sharp *pinga,* the Indians' crude brandy, that the trader sold. He was quite sure they'd both be stuck

here for the rest of the day, and the next day, and that the
launch would sail back to the distant coastal city without
them. *Stuck here,* he was thinking, *in this damned jungle
with nothing to do except loose off casual shots at casual
animals. And miss them,* he thought. He said sullenly, "That
damned launch won't wait for us, you know."

And then the outboard motor roared, sending a reboant,
unexpected sound echoing through the forest. The older
man said triumphantly, "What did I tell you? A fouled-up
plug is all. Let's go."

The young man picked up the *pinga* bottle quickly and
drank the last drop from it and tossed it into the river, and
then splashed his way into the white-painted boat; the paint
was peeling off all down its length, exposing the rotting
boards underneath.

And when it shot out into midstream and became part of
the fast-flowing current, he did not even look back at the
shore. He did not even glance at the rocks that towered over
the banks of the river, covered splendidly with dark and
light and medium greens. Against the foliage, three huge
butterflies, bright blue *borboletas,* more than eight inches
across from wingtip to wingtip, were shimmering with a
startling incandescence; he did not see them.

Up on the rock, far away downwind, Bichu was
watching. There was a pool of dark-red blood below her
mouth, and from time to time her stomach shuddered, and
the soft, furry flank trembled; and sometimes there was a
great fear of death on her, because, although death was so
easily acceptable in the forest, she had never before known

that it would be so acutely painful. She looked, uncomprehending, at the caulked blood on her chest; and she tried to
lick it. But the movement of her head merely brought up
more blood, and she spluttered once to clear her mouth of
the froth, and let her body roll over without any conscious
effort to fight it, letting a dangerous lassitude seep over her.

She had heard, with alarm, the sudden roar of the outboard motor; it had sounded to her like a gunshot, multi-
plied a million times over, and it had meant to her that
more of the pain would overwhelm her. For the first time
in her life she knew terror. And when the pain did not
come, she still steeled herself against it and waited. At last
she began to cough again, uncontrollably, knowing that the
sound could bring new danger, but unable to stifle it.

The sound of the motor died away, and soon there were
only the accustomed noises of the jungle; she could not
know what the cessation of the frightening sound meant;
she could only hope that it meant that an unidentified
danger had passed.

There was a heavy fluttering in the branches of the tree
above her, and she looked up; a vulture.

She transferred her gaze back to the wisp of smoke, still
smoldering, down there in the valley, listening for the unaccustomed sounds. She went on watching, for a long, long
time. The heat of the day went, and the pandemonium of
the forest grew louder; and as the twilight fell, she forced
a new movement into her stiffened limbs and haltingly
crawled away toward the mountains, where the sun had set,
acutely conscious of the way her easy movements had stiffened and slowed, so that all her feline grace had gone. She
was staggering brokenly, a dying animal, pathetic in her
loneliness and incomprehension. Behind her the patient
vulture dropped down heavily from the tree and began to

peck at the dried blood she had left behind her. She paused, the pain racking her body, and turned to look back; there were three of them now, and one of them was watching her with cruel, beady eyes.

She found, unaccountably, that she was lying flat on her side. She fought against the torpor and struggled to her feet again, knowing that her right shoulder was useless now. She limped away into the darkness, moving clumsily, falling, dragging herself along by an effort of instinct and will; she had a long way, a very long way, to go. And there was only that will to carry her there. If not all the way, at least as far as she could go toward the place that was her territory, her home.

The wind changed and brought back the sound of the boat. It was distant now, and receding, and she listened till she was sure that it had gone forever, taking with it the terribly casual menace that had rendered her helpless and then, as casually, left her to suffer.

One danger, she knew, was gone; but it had left her fearfully vulnerable to so many others.

chapter two

The night had come, and Bichu shivered.

It was time for food, but she had thrust all thought of eating away from her; the throbbing pains in her stomach would allow her to think of nothing but the tearing of soft flesh inside her every time she moved; she crept with an instinct of desperation, always down, down the steep slope and away from the rocks which would serve as a barrier between her and the dreadful danger that lay beyond them, the danger that she knew only as a sibilant, frightening voice out of the forest that meant death to her.

The pain was constant. But sometimes it suddenly rose to a peak, and once she lay on her back and struggled to hang on to her consciousness, knowing that this was not the place to die because it was too far from the friendly things of her childhood.

And when she thought of this, there was an animal stubbornness in her that drove her on again, drove her to forget the tearing pains. She limped on three legs, her right foreleg curled up under her chest; sometimes she stopped

to lick the blood off it, not knowing whether the blood came from her mouth or from her shoulder. Once, accidentally, she stumbled into a small stream, and the icy cold of it was a comfort to her. She rested awhile, coughing in the darkness, coughing out the frothy blood which clung to her muzzle. And then she moved on again, unsteadily, remembering the agility she used to have and not quite sure why it was no longer with her.

It was the hunting time for her too, and she could smell the tempting scents of food all around her; she could hear the rustle as an antelope pushed through the trees, and instinctively she moved downwind of it. But her movements were clumsy now, and the antelope heard her and raced away, its pointed ears up, its bright eyes wide with fright. She made an instinctive leap toward it and whimpered when the agony struck her with the movement; and now she lost consciousness completely.

For a long time she lay where she had fallen, not hidden as she should have been, but carelessly half-exposed in a patch of bright moonlight; and when she awoke at last, a long dark-brown snake was crawling over her body, seeking her warmth on its belly; it would not harm her, she knew, but the slithering of its scales over her fur revolted her. She tried to reach out to it with her right paw and push it away, but she could not move. She rolled over, doubling herself up (bringing back the pain), and dragged herself away from it; the snake turned its head to look at her and then went on its way.

She wondered why it had shown no fear; was her helplessness so easy to see? In her long sleep the blood had congealed around her mouth again, and she rubbed it hard against the wet moss she was lying on, and when the sweet taste of it had gone, she stumbled blindly on, heading always down the hillside, moving wearily, knowing that it was a long, long way to go and that there were many obstacles to overcome before she could comfortably lie down and let death sweep over her and take away the pain.

She was cold now, because she could not move with her accustomed speed; she thought about the river that was at the bottom of the mountain, a river she had to swim over, and when she heard the sound of the water, it was a comfort to her because she knew that, pain or no pain, conscious or in a coma, her sense of direction was still good.

In her mind she could see the major landmarks: the river, the steep cliff on the other side with the light sandstone bluff above it (a bluff that she must climb in the darkness, or in the late afternoon—at any time when the sun was not striking it and casting dark shadows of anything that moved across it). And then the open plain, a vast long stretch of almost treeless scrub that offered too little cover for safety and must be crossed at speed; here, too, she was thinking, she must move only in the darkness. At other times she would have been contemptuous of the danger, trusting implicitly to her great speed, to her agility, to the ease with which she could slip like a shadow under the shade of the smallest bush.

And now, with the thought of the plain, there was an ancient memory nagging at her mind, for in Bichu's world all memories were lessons that must never be forgotten, for the forgetting could be fatal; she lay down to rest for a while, shivering, and tried to bring it into focus. (A long time ago, crossing this plain, the pampas, she had been chased by a group of horsemen, eight or nine gauchos who had been roaming far in their search for a lost pony. Swinging their bolas around their heads, whooping their delight, they had chased her across the plain. But her speed was too much for them, and so was her cunning and she had easily eluded them.)

The pampas, she knew, were a danger. She pushed the thought of it into the recesses at the back of her mind; she would take it out again when the time came, remembering, never forgetting the lessons.

But now, now there was the river to worry about. It was deep, she remembered, and running fast, with the white waters curling up over half-submerged rocks, rushing fast on its way to the great falls farther downstream. There was a heavy overhang of broken branches that leaned drunkenly from the near bank and almost, but not quite, reached the other side. She remembered that once she had crossed this way when she had found the waters infested with the hunting piranhas, gathering in immense and deadly shoals. She had watched them feeding on a small deer she had been stalking at the river's edge; she had heard the panic-stricken screams, and then she had wondered at the sudden silence, broken only by the thrashing in the water.

She had crossed over, then, by the overhead branches, leaping the last twenty feet and landing in the soft yellow mud where the crocodiles were basking, half-submerged to keep the dangerous sun off their thick but delicate skins. But now . . . could she climb the tree with her mutilated muscles? Could she make that leap to the other side? She thought not.

But she would have to try. She moved on, limping heavily, dragging herself along from tree to tree, slithering over the wet humus, pushing herself through the foliage with strong hindlegs, and grinding her teeth against the pain. And at last she came to the river.

The sound of it was comforting; it was a step nearer her home. Unerringly, she had come straight to the place where

the broken trees were. She crouched under a bush that was
eerily purple and light green in the white glow of the moon,
looking up at the branches. More of them had fallen since
last she passed this way, and she examined them carefully,
for a long and patient time, before she decided that she
would have to swim.

She eased herself out from the shelter and stood, on three
legs, watching the waters and waiting. She stretched her long
body and tried to move her right shoulder, trying to force
some response from the rigid, useless leg, watching all the
while the surface of the water for the sudden bursts of fury
which were the telltale sign of the deadly fish; there was
silence.

And then she heard a slight sporadic coughing sound, a
short, sharp, muffled hiccuping. Curiously, she turned her
head in the direction of the sound; it was a long way away.
Again instinct told her what to do—explore, and weigh the
danger there.

She began to creep toward it silently, watching her every
step every inch of the way. She crept through the tangle of
vines that shielded her from sight, under the rotting logs,
silently onto a fallen tree, across which a giant fern was
trailing, and down again onto a small clearing by the water,
where the grass was wet and therefore silent to her movements. Ahead of her a pile of leafy humus had been gathered, a yard high and twice as wide, and it was giving off a
strong and fishlike scent that stirred the hunger pains
again.

Now, with the hiccuping, there was a faint cracking
sound. Deep in the pile of leaves there was a clutch of crocodile eggs, and the young were bursting out of their shells,
cracking them open with the tiny egg-teeth that would soon,
once they were free, drop away from the long and slender

snouts. The hiccuping sound was growing stronger each minute; there would be twenty or thirty eggs there, perhaps more. It was a source of food she did not much like, but she knew too that ahead of her lay a long, long period of hunger; how could she hunt with the pain tearing at her every time she moved? And if she could not hunt how could she survive?

She looked to the east and saw that there was already a red streak in the sky. Soon the day and the dangers of the daylight would be coming, and her shattered belly should be full of nourishing food to help her fight off the nausea and the weariness. . . . .

She began to stalk the nest, wary of the dangers around it; not the dangers of the young crocodiles, who would snap at her uselessly, but the greater danger that lurked nearby. Somewhere, not too far away, the mother would be watching her young, waiting for the shell-cracking to finish so that she could call her brood to her lair by imitating their sounds. The mother would be deep in the mud, the flaps of her ears open for the slightest sound.

Silence, then . . .

Bichu crept forward.

When she reached the nest, she tried to reach out with one foreleg to sweep away some of the leaves. She made small, hopping movements, trying to use the only front leg she could stand on. And then, suddenly, there was a violent rush of sound behind her. She spun around, moving too fast and falling to the ground in pain, her teeth bared and her eyes alight with alarm as the great crocodile, twelve feet long and flaying its huge tail, came hurtling toward her. There was time to see that the scent-glands at each side of the long scaly throat were red and swollen, turned inside out with the fury. (When the crocodiles were basking, or swimming, or at peace with their own primeval world, you could not see these glands at all. But when that prehistoric fury came over them, the glands gathered and curled and turned red like obscene and fleshy slashes along the throat; it was part of an age-old world that had died a million years ago, and it meant great danger.)

And then the great reptile was on her, the huge mouth open, the sharp teeth slashing. Bichu drove hard with her rear legs and sent herself flying along the ground, ripping with her sharp teeth at the lower snout as she went past it. And then she was suddenly, unaccountably, on her back with nausea sweeping over her, and the crocodile was turning, the short stubby legs firmly anchored, the monstrous tail raised high to one side.

She saw the great mass of it coming down at her and tried to swing away from it. But simultaneously with the movement she tried to make, a white-hot pain coursed through her stomach and paralyzed her, and then the tail hit her and she squealed her agony as it thudded into her, sending her spinning helplessly toward the water. She heard a great bellow which she knew was a male nearby, and as she tried to turn over in the wet and sticky mud she saw the churning waters as an angry snout, the beady eyes bright behind it, came streaking fast toward her. She tried to run, but in the mud she could only slither.

And then the water was alive with them, thrashing around her, trying to reach her before she could find her feet again. Desperately she tried to overcome the pain; she bit into her tongue and struggled for the shore and threw herself sideways as a great gaping mouth snapped shut like a steel trap close to her head.

A branch was close above her, and she struggled to reach it, hearing again the sound of the snapping jaws that could have taken her leg off like a knife; and then she was clear of the ground, pumping blood out of her mouth and coughing through the froth of it. Her soft belly was heaving as she strained for more air, and as she moved higher to better safety she slipped on her own vomit and wrapped a foreleg around the branch for security, struggling to keep her balance.

Below her the sharp eyes were watching her; she crawled painfully along the heavy branch and lay there awhile, coughing, making the sounds that were dangerous even in the night—and the day was coming fast now—but unable to restrain herself. She could feel that her eyes were glazing over again, clouding her vision, and she knew that if she lost her consciousness she would fall; she wrapped her good leg tighter around the branch and dug the sharp claws of her rear paws into the bark, holding tight grimly till the paroxysm should pass.

At last she raised her head and searched the branches of the tree she was in. She crawled laboriously to the limb's extremity, testing it carefully for strength as she moved; and when she had gone as far as she could, she lay close with her belly touching the bark for the whole length of her body and looked across at the other side of the river; it seemed a terribly long way to leap, even had she been at her strongest; but she feared the water now; there was too much blood. She remembered the fish, and she knew also that she could not swim fast enough to outstrip the crocodiles if, excited now, they should come after her. In her present incapacitated state she was too easy a prey for them. They would fasten their great teeth on her and drag her down under the water; and there they would thrust her dead body into hollows in the banks and let her decompose till she was ripe enough to satisfy their filthy appetites.

She did not stop to think anymore, because in thought there was indecision. She gritted her teeth, took a deep breath, and leaped out into the void.

One paw stretched out in front of her, the other dangling uselessly, she landed on her side' in the water, and 'the shock of pain almost overcame her; she struck out blindly, hearing the churning water behind her, pumping her back legs hard and trying not to feel the throbbing pain inside her. Her mouth was filled with water and blood, and she could hear the grinding of her own shattered ribs.

All down her left side now, the crushing blow of the crocodile's tail could still be felt, and with each desperate movement the edges .of shattered bone were scraping, sending arrows of fire through her body. But .her rear legs were still good, and she felt the wet riverbed under them; and then she was on the land, dragging herself on her side through the mud, scraping her way to the ferns that were thick there, burrowing deep among them, twisting her head first to one side and then the other, searching out any new dangers that might lurk there.

There was a pool of cool water, and a solitary fish was struggling in the shallows, trying to reach the river again, and instinctively, craving the food, she reached out a paw and tried to catch it. The pain shot through her with each movement, but she was training herself now to overcome it. And then the broad claws found their mark, and she scooped the fish into her mouth, chewing on it hungrily, as if she knew that in nourishment there were a few more hours of life, a few more hours in which to reach her home.

Was it an obsession? She could not know. All she knew was that at all costs she must get away from the river and tackle the next great obstacle, the steep bluff she would have to climb in the darkness.

But the day had come now, the first gray light streaking through the trees; soon the steam would be rising from the wet foliage as the heat of the sun uncurled the leaves, and the time would come when a hunted animal must find shelter from the frightful, cruel dangers that were all around it.

She thought again of the sandstone bluff and of the darkness she would need. But first she must reach it, and she must rest nearby so that she could tackle it when her strength returned. There, on the edge of the valley, close under the bluff, she would sleep; here sleep would be too dangerous.

She looked up into the foliage, searching patiently. Soon she saw the vultures. They had followed her in the darkness and were waiting. If she lay down here and let the alertness go, even for a few moments, the ugly birds would tumble clumsily down beside her, watch her for a while to make sure she was helpless . . . and then, first they would peck out her eyes, quickly and skillfully, before they began to tear at her living flesh with their great curved beaks, so strong that they could cut a bone in two without effort.

She willed herself to move, slowly and in cruel pain, deep in among the trees. Somewhere there, closer to the bluff on the other side, she would find a hollow tree trunk she could crawl into, a cave perhaps, or even a thornbush that would keep her enemies away.

Sleep. Sleep. . . . But not here.

She struggled on. The full moon rose high, spreading a ghostly light across the tops of the trees. But below them the darkness was absolute.

chapter three

When the sun rose across the glorious plain, it seemed as though the green land were touched with gold. The purple shadow crept slowly down the slopes of the distant mountains like a living thing as the night receded into the earth.

Against the bright-blue sky, so clear and clean, with a few scattered clouds that drifted aimlessly, the gently curved horizon had the form of a sleeping woman; you could clearly see the rise of her breast, the smooth undulation of her stomach, the slight elevation of a raised knee; there was even a small forest of lacy trees where her hair would be, and at the other extremity a pinnacle of ancient rock rose up like a pointed toe; and the silence added to the illusion. The mission Indians called the range *a moça que cai no sono*, "the girl who fell asleep."

"*A moça*," they would say, "became tired one day, many ages gone, when she was looking for her lover in the mountains. She fell asleep, and one day her lover will return to her, and then the girl will awaken. . . ."

The mountains rimmed a great green valley, and at one side, to the south, the valley fell away again into a huge broken crevasse where a river flowed fast at the bottom, where tall wild para trees grew, which the Indians would sometimes tap for rubber, squatting patiently like animals in the shadows till the white sap had filled their wicker baskets, and then carrying them on their heads down the riverbank, cautiously, because they did not like to travel too far from the security of their own territory, which, like the animals, they regarded as their own by heritage. Some of them, the ones who had been to the missions, would even boil the latex in earthenware pots, because then the price was always a few pennies higher, and with the money they could buy rusted old nails and bolts to beat into arrowheads or tips for their spears.

The Indians were so few in number, in so immense a land. They tended to hide even from each other, skulking silently in the bushes like animals and knowing that the whole world was their enemy. For hundreds and hundreds of miles in all directions there was nothing; and then, unaccountably, you would see the thin smoke of their cooking fires in the distance. And yet, if you went there to take a closer look, you would find nothing, because they would have heard your slightest sound and gone, gone quickly deeper into the forest, leaving only their ashes and the hot stones and the ephemeral smoke.

Sometimes whole villages, villages of forty or fifty or even a hundred souls, would be emptied completely overnight, just because a strange sound had been heard or a column of blue smoke that was not their own had been seen; there would be nothing left but a few rickety, empty, silent huts, and cooking stones, and broken wicker baskets, and scattered patterns of hollowed-out cups in the sand where the silent children had once played the game with the pebbles. And if you looked deeper in the jungle, still searching for the frightened men, you would still find nothing; for they would retreat before you, gathering up their nothings and moving away. . . .

A path led crazily down the steep sandstone bluff from the tiny village that was perched on the hill, well away from the river; it was perched up there, even though it meant a long walk for the women in the dry season, when the river was the only source of water, because many years ago, when the village was first built, it had been necessary to find a certain security from the tribe upstream, who used the river as a means of assault, raiding their neighbors for *mandioca* when their own crop failed or when they had been too busy fighting to plant any; or raiding for weapons, or sometimes for women, or sometimes simply because war was their constant way of life.

So the village was perched up on the thick-forested mountain, and in the summer the women would wander down the steep bluff in groups of ten or twelve, with earthenware pots on their hips or hung from straps slung around their tattooed foreheads, bending their backs under the heavy loads on the way up again. Even so, sometimes the neighbors would be there, lying in wait for them; and it had thus become a custom that only the older women would fetch water, because the younger ones were highly prized among the river raiders, whom the villagers called "*Os desatitos*," which meant in their dialect "The greedy ones."

And, for the villagers, the *desatitos* were not the only danger. For their land, so remote in time and distance from any kind of civilization but their own, had recently fallen prey to a new plague; it was what they called in the distant

cities "*desenvolvimento*," the opening up of the ancient
forest spaces to make room for new farms to feed the millions
of a hungry continent.

The villagers would creep out of their forest huts and
watch with awe as great machines swooped down out of the
sky with other machines inside them, machines that roared
like angry crocodiles, but a thousand times louder, and
crashed through the scrub to tear down the trees that had
always given them shelter. The Indians would crouch in
terror, shivering at the very size and power of these monstrous machines, growing ever nearer, even when they
walked days and days deeper into the forests; there seemed
no way to escape.

And worse, sometimes a distant landowner, so far away
that his name was never known, would send out a team
of gauchos with a terrible mission—to wipe out any scattered, lonely Indians they might find there, because
the Indians, who still hunted one another with poisoned
arrows and cut off each other's heads for pleasure, were a
danger to the foreigners who would come from distant
states to claim these lands as their own. And so the gauchos
would ride the plains with their deadly bolas and their
knives, and sometimes even guns, and the terrified Indians
would once more pull back, still deeper into their jungle;
those who survived the massacres, that is. . . .

Deeper and deeper they went into the limitless jungle;
someday, some of them knew, there would be no more
jungle for them to hide in, for however big it was—and it
had always seemed to them to be without any kind of limit,
even though a man should walk through it more days than
he could count—there was always the fear that the machines
would drive them into other tribal territories where they
would be killed. There was so little of human life here,
and so much of death.

But now, looking at the hills as the shadows dropped slowly from them, disclosing all their ancient glory, you could not imagine that here there could be anything but the most perfect peace. The gold was creeping over the foothills, and the dark shadows were long and graceful under the tall green trees that were climbing the slopes, and the bushes, thickly clustered, were a bright green carpet spreading over the ground that was still moist and steaming with the night's dew.

The smoke was spiraling up, the blue smoke that was the ubiquitous sign of lonely human intrusion into the wilderness. Under the shelter of a huge fleshy tree whose leaves hung pendulously down, filled with sap and shining brightly in the sun, an Indian stirred in his red-and-brown blanket. He lay curled up tightly with the blanket bunched around his shoulders, and he opened a dark eye to see, with appreciation, that the girl was carefully pouring a few drops of burning *pinga* into the tin pot that held the coffee; it was the scent of the coffee that had awakened him.

She was slight, and small, and not much more than twelve years old, but a woman already. She wore a crude shift of printed cotton in bright colors and a blanket-cape over her bare shoulders, and she turned and smiled when she saw that her father was awake. With a bare foot she stirred the embers of the small fire, and she placed the tin pot carefully at the edge of the hot stones; her movements were very slow and deliberate, unhurried.

The Indian looked at her as he stretched his cramped limbs, and he was thinking: *One day, soon now, my daughter will make a fine wife for some lucky boy from the tribe; or perhaps she will go to the mission and learn to read, and then to the city and work, and she will send home money for her father. She is very pretty, my daughter, and she will make a fine bride and bring me a great credit.*

The city, for the Indian, was an ugly cluster of white-washed houses forty miles up the river, where he had been only twice in his life. The launch that carried the raw rubber downriver called there every month. In the city they made a crude whiskey from bananas, and there was even a café where a man could sit and watch the river and dream away the whole day if he had a few cruzeiros in his pocket or was prepared to cut wood for the launch for a few hours.

He thought of himself, this Indian, as a civilized man, far better and more cultured than most of his kind, for whom he had a kind of tolerant contempt (except for the *desatitos*, whom he feared greatly).

He was civilized because his family had once lived for a long time in one of the missions the kindly Fathers had put up on the edge of the forest, offering food and hoping to tempt more of the tribesmen into their strange new ways. He had learned to speak their language, which they had taught to his daughter, because he had seen that this language, Portuguese, was the strange tongue the solitary traders spoke when they came through the forest, seeking out skins, or baskets of rubber, or panniers of nuts, or jars of oil, or anything else that they could buy for a handful of cruzeiros or trade in exchange for iron nails, or cloth, or the strong rope the foreigners used. He thought it would be useful if his daughter could speak this language as well, because then she could find work in the missions when there was no food to be had in the villages. And in this, in that he thought about it at all, he was indeed more cultured than the rest of them, who had nothing but scorn and fear for the white men, even though they saw them very, very rarely, not more than once or twice in the course of a year.

He wore a loincloth around his waist and carried a blanket; and sometimes he wore beads around his neck and a brightly colored feather strapped to his ankle, although the Fathers had told him (a piece of information he doubted) that it would not really keep the evil spirits away.

He was short and stubby and immensely strong, but he was a kind and gentle man, gentle enough to be deeply concerned about his daughter, because he instinctively knew that the world she would have to face would be very different from the comforting world he himself had always known; there were disturbing signs that the world was changing faster than he would have liked. For this reason he had almost given up his native dialect, not realizing that this was a frantic and useless effort to become part of that new world. He spoke Portuguese to his daughter, struggling with a language that was too rich for his simple needs in an effort to bridge the gap that was between them, even though it was desperately hard for him. For the minds of the very young, the change was so much easier.

His name was Urubelava, which in the language of his villagers meant "The stubborn man."

He got up now and wrapped his blanket over his shoulders and crouched over the embers of the fire and sipped the coffee the girl gave him, silently, and looked at her while she packed up their few belongings and wrapped the string around them into a convenient bundle for her head. There was not much to carry. The enameled pot that was used for cooking, or for carrying water, or for making dyes ... a piece of string he had made, a stronger piece of rope, a little cloth bag for coffee beans, an old soft-drink bottle a trader had given him in which they carried the *pinga* (it was stoppered with a piece of rag), a few spare arrowheads, an extra blanket, a piece of sharpening-stone that was always getting lost and replaced. Their needs were very few.

When he had finished, he handed her the pot to tie onto the bundle, and he restrung the little bow that he had carefully unstrung against the damp of the night, and he examined the bundle of arrows meticulously and checked that they were still straight, tensing one of them that had become a little warped by holding it between his feet and putting pressure on it with his hands till it was straight as a die again, and then he stood up and said, "Well."

She knew that he meant the coffee was good, and she smiled quickly, showing very white teeth. Her eyes were large and dark and solemn and bright, and her bones were finely formed. There was a white man's blood in her somewhere, white blood he had seen when he took her mother in the year of the great migration.

This foreign blood was no shame. On the contrary, it had given both the mother and the daughter a certain prestige in the tribe. A sailor from the launch, the mother had said proudly, had been her father, a huge pink-colored man with black hair and a beard, who spoke Portuguese with a strange accent and had never bothered to learn the local tongue, contenting himself with grunted orders to her in pidgin. She too, like her daughter, was tall and slim, without any of the dumpiness of the other women, with long legs that were unusually straight, like those of the white women at the mission. They had called the daughter Marina, because the men of the launch were called *marineros*, and her name, they thought, should be a permanent reminder of the great honor that was theirs in the sailor's blood.

He stood waiting for her while she adjusted the necklace of shells that he had given her, looking back at her admiringly, two lone figures a hundred miles from anywhere. He turned and looked at the valley and at the distant line of dark 'green that marked the drop down to the river, and he said, "Three days more, and then we will return. And for this work, they will give me cloth, and a leather bag, and some iron to make arrowheads with; it is good business."

She nodded, knowing the cloth would be hers to make a dress with, her eyes lighting up at the thought of it. She said, laughing, "Red cloth. It must be red."

He nodded gravely. "Red, and purple, and yellow, like the flowers on the side of the mountain."

She clapped her hands with a delighted childlike gesture, and they moved off together toward the distant green. It was wild and unknown country he was going to for the first time, and he was a little worried about the people, if any, he might find there. "There are no people," they had told him; "there is nothing to fear."

But he could not be sure. He remembered the *desatitos* and worried about his daughter. But his woman had said, "Take the child with you; I am too old to travel so far. It is time she learned to care for a man."

The elders of his tribe, who were the Arasuyas of the great valley, had nodded wisely and agreed: "There are no people there, there is nothing to fear."

And the work, he knew, was not too complicated. It was a question of counting the para trees a man could walk past in one day along the bank of the river, because somewhere, far away, some unknown *chefe* wanted to take the latex from them for sale to the merchants in the city. The Indian had brought a flat piece of susu bark with him, and when he reached the river he would make charcoal and use it to mark down the trees on the piece of bark—a line for every tree, they had told him. It was a great responsibility, and it was this responsibility, secretly, that had

made him accept the offer; this, more than the leather bag
and the cloth, or even the iron for the arrows, which he
sorely needed.

He said again, "Two more days, daughter."

She laughed delightedly. "And the cloth, will it be
enough for a dress?"

"More than enough. If they are good men, it will be
more than enough."

Fifteen or twenty of the young men from the village
were fanning out to count the trees, some of them traveling
as far as eight days' walk away, and eight was almost more
than a man could count.

When the sun rose higher and they had been padding
along for more than four hours on bare feet, he took off his
blanket and tossed it to her to carry and said solicitously
(because he was very fond of her), "If you are tired, we will
rest for a while."

But, thinking of the cloth, she shook her head. They
moved on, in silence. Because of the heat, she had slipped
the shift down from her shoulders and tied it around her
waist with string. Her father looked proudly at her and
thought: *A woman already, and soon I must find her a
husband in the tribe; with the cloth, and the iron for the
arrows, it will be easy.*

The heat of the bright sun pounded down on their
shining brown bodies. They were so much alone, the two
of them, in so vast a country.

It was the heat of the sun that woke Bichu.

With a sudden start she realized that she should have
awakened long ago, and for a brief moment she could not

understand why she had slept so long and so dangerously. But when she began, instinctively, to stretch her long limbs, all the terrible memories came back with the rush of pain. When she yelped, the caked blood on her mouth cracked with a soft, unlikely sound, and she began to drag herself into a position that would, perhaps, ease the pain a little. It was mounting now, filling the whole of her insides, and there was a dull, insistent ache down the side of her ribs.

She remembered the *jacares*, the crocodiles, with a mixture of fear and triumph. She recalled the leap she had made, first up into the tree—but that was her instinct driving her beyond the limits of animal endeavor—and then the calculated bound across the water to the other bank, and the desperate struggle in the water. She could smell again the sour stench of the clutch of eggs, hear again the hiccuping sounds. But now the tiny reptiles would be with their mother in her lair, already vicious, already angry with the rest of a hostile world.

Her bright brown-and-yellow eyes were searching everywhere, checking the security of the lair she had found to sleep in. A wet and slimy log lay close over her back, supported by a jagged stump, lichen-covered, that was interwoven with a brilliant green creeper splashed here and there with crimson blossoms. A clump of old bamboo that would rustle if even a lizard moved there hid a tiny enclosure, and behind her there was the comforting feel of solid gray rock.

She moved forward an inch or two, scenting, listening, watching; nothing moved. She could hear the shrill cries of parrots up in the treetops, and she watched for a while as the foolish birds fluttered their bright colors as they preened themselves. She watched a pair of iridescent butterflies. She searched for the vultures; had they gone?

She could smell the scent of fresh blood, and it was not her own. She listened, turning her head slowly to peer through the bamboo; there was the faintest crushing sound there. . . . She snarled once, angrily, and the sound stopped. And then a monstrous bird flew up out of the long grass, a bird more than three feet high, with a cruel hooked beak and bright-gray plumage that was dappled with gray and black; two great feathered crests stood up high above its white nightmare face, and in its strong claws it clutched the remains of a dead and bloodied monkey. It was the great harpy eagle, and as Bichu watched, it soared high above her head, its meal still held tight in those steel claws, and wheeled away toward the mountains.

She knew then that the vultures were no longer there, not near enough to tempt the martial anger of the eagle, nor its voracious appetite.

She moved out farther. The sound of water was nearby, and she wondered why she had not heard it when she lay down to rest. The wind had moved then. She moved slightly into it, carefully, around the noisy bamboo, and now she could see the bluff, not too far away, with the sun bright on its brilliant ocher surface.

There was a dark shadow at its base, a shadow stretching up and to one side—a crevasse; she remembered it well. Above the crevasse a patch of sunlight, and then a clump of dried-out thorns. Above the thorns, another bare patch of danger, and then deep shadows again, where a tiny gully that sometimes carried water was overgrown with tangled grasses. At the top of the valley there was a long, low overhang with shadows beneath it, and then a level patch of soft sand that would betray her presence with the pad marks she would leave on it. And then, once more, the shade of an outcrop that was fast creeping away from the sun. Her sharp, wary eyes examined every detail, measuring the dangers.

The soft sand worried her. But could she, if need be, find shelter under the overhang? Could she stay there till the sun swung around and let her climb the rest of the way in shadow? She thought perhaps she could.

But first . . . She had passed the night with only one small fish to eat, and her stomach was craving more nourishment. Without food there is no strength. She began to creep, very slowly, toward the sound of the water. She checked the wind again and moved to one side to bring her downwind of it, and on the breeze she could detect an alien scent; an antelope? The saliva began to rise in her mouth, and she crept on, her belly close to the ground, her long tail switching ever so slightly. She tried her bad leg and found again that she still could not use it; but her hind legs were strong, the killing legs that could rip and slash like steel knives.

She moved on. And when she came to the tiny stream she was glad her senses, clouded over with pain, had not deceived her; a *suasupucu*, the marsh deer, was watering there, the ten points of his horns lowered, the chestnut skin shining in the sunlight.   . . .

Bichu could hear the gentle sound of the lapping water as the deer drank. She watched for a long time, her eyes immobile except when once or twice she glanced sharply to the side to check the constant sounds and smells that were all around her, with no unwelcome intrusion to catch her unawares. Her pink tongue played with her lips; the hunger was very strong.

And then the deer raised his head in alarm, and she tensed her muscles and leaped forward, one single paw outstretched for the long neck, the killing legs ready to reach into the underside of the sleek body. She felt the pains shooting through her stomach again as she leaped, and in an effort to still them she twisted in midair and landed on her back, close by, pawing the wind, her lips drawn back in agony, her eyes dulled. And when she recovered from the shock the deer had gone; she had not even heard it crashing through the bushes, and she knew that the stabbing pain that had robbed her of her senses had also robbed her of her instinct for caution; how long had she lain there unconscious? The blood was oozing out of her mouth, and she was very much weaker.

She stumbled to her feet and moved on unsteadily, heading for the bluff, not thinking of the wind, not thinking of the scents around her, not thinking of the sounds of the forest; there was only one thought: home. Even the thought of food, and the realization that if she could not hunt she could not eat, seemed, at this moment, to be of no importance.

When she reached the great sandstone cliff, she looked up to the top, far higher above her than it had ever seemed before. Her breath was short and painful; her tongue was hanging out; her body was sagging. Slowly, laboriously, she ground her teeth together and began the long climb.

Inch by inch, step by painful step, she dragged herself over the steep hot sand, dragging her belly, slipping sometimes and clutching at the earth with her good front paw for support. Once she fell back and rolled over and over down to the bottom, but when her breath had returned her animal stubbornness helped her on the way up again.

And soon she came to a wide, flat place where the rain had carved out a small valley; there was thick brush growing there, and there were friendly grasses, still cool and damp in the shade from the night's dew. She dragged herself into it, panting, laboring, and could go no farther; she lay down to rest; and soon the coma swept over her again and all the pain and the consciousness and the awareness of what was happening to her were mercifully swept aside.

The two Indians, the man and the girl, were moving down.

The man swung by its yellow feet a small jungle turkey, a *curassow*, that he had killed with his bow for the midday meal. He had stopped to let the girl rest, and when he had heard the birds nearby calling to each other in their deep, resonant honk, he had imitated the sound by cupping his hand to his mouth and calling with a softly cooing sound; one of the birds had wandered over, snapping its head high from time to time, to the hiding place he had chosen; and while the girl watched, her eyes sparkling, he had shot it through the neck with his first shaft.

Now he was idly plucking off the feathers as he walked. He cut off the feathered crest with his knife and tossed it to her and said, "For your hair."

In a little while they found a broad ledge on the side of the bluff where a gray slab of granite gave shade from the hot sun, and he threw the bird to the girl and went off to find wood to make fire with, using a dry stick which he twirled with his bowstring to start the flames; and while he was blowing on the sparks, crouched over the wood with his bony knees upthrust, the girl went off to one side to take the offal out of the bird and clean it, tearing it neatly into two parts, the bigger one for her father and the smaller one for herself.

But soon she came running back, her eyes bright with excitement. She said breathlessly: "*Jaguar tirica*, an ocelot." There was blood on her long brown fingers from the bird, and her father looked up sharply and asked: "Where?"

She pointed "Tracks, in the soft sand, there."

He got up at once, leaving the fire and quickly restringing his bow; he had already fitted an arrow to it when he dropped down to his haunches and laid a delicate finger on the pad marks, touching them lightly and shifting the sand to test its density. He said, "Not an ocelot, a jaguar." He struggled to remember the word and said, "An *onca*, a jaguar. It is a small one, a female, and she walks on three legs, and there is blood; she has been hurt." He pulled at his thick lip, reading the signs and puzzling them out methodically, and said at last, "She has had a fight, and I think it was with a *jacare*."

The girl's eyes were wide at her father's assurance. "A *jacare*, a crocodile? Here, so far from the water?

"Down there, by the river." Seeing her puzzlement, he said, "The blood is dark; it comes from inside the body. That means that some animal has crushed her. If it were a snake—a boa or an anaconda—she would not have survived. So, it must have been a crocodile; there is no other animal that could harm her so. And it was not very long ago. When we have eaten our food, we will follow it. I think it is moving very slowly."

Delighted, she asked, "A skin to sell?"

He shook his head gravely. "No, better than a skin." He stood up and scratched at his chin with a calloused hand and said slowly, trying to remember, "A long time ago, in the city, there was a merchant, a man who sold things to people. One of my friends had a baby coati, a tame one that he had kept in his house for a long long time. It would take food from his children's hands. . . ."

He was secretly pleased that he could find a reason to talk so much with his daughter, instructing her. He fingered the blue tattoo marks on his face, his dark eyes shining, and said carefully, "Well, my friend sold the coati to this man, who gave him a *facao*, a long knife, for it. This man said that he would buy any animals my friend could bring him, to take to the zoo on the coast, a long way away. You understand what I am saying? The man will buy, for money, any animal we can bring him." He added gravely, "'A zoo, a place where they keep animals in cages for people to look at. He said he would pay much money for a jaguar, more than a thousand cruzeiros, if it was alive."

Her eyes widened. "A thousand cruzeiros? What would you do with so much money?"

He shook his head. "I do not know." He thought for a while and said stubbornly, "I only know that with a thousand cruzeiros I would be a wealthy man, the wealthiest in the village. The others would respect me greatly because of it. We will follow the jaguar, and I will catch it."

The girl said firmly, "One man alone cannot catch a jaguar."

"This one has only three legs; she cannot run very fast. And she is wounded. I will make a net of vines which you will fetch for me, and then . . ."

He broke off, wondering what the next step would be. He knew that if merchants bought live animals, then there must be a way of catching them, but he did not know what it was, and he did not want to admit that he did not know. There must be a way, he was thinking. He had heard of young cubs being taken from their lairs before they were old enough to run far, but this . . .

He said, "Then I will find a way to get it into the net, and we will tie its feet, and we will take it back to the village with us. And I will send a boy to the city to tell the merchant I have a good jaguar for him if he will send the money." He nodded, convincing himself. "That is how it will be."

"And the trees? Counting the trees?"

He shrugged. "Another day, another two days, it does not matter." He said again, nodding violently, "That is how it will be."

They cooked the fowl over the fire with a stick through the two pieces, and when they had eaten it, tearing off the juicy flesh with their fingers, they left the fire there and started to follow the spoor.

They walked in single file, very slowly, with the man in front, watching for the pad marks and sometimes dropping to the ground when they were hard to see, with the girl a few paces behind him, marveling at the ease with which he could pick up the tracks. *My father is a splendid man,* she was thinking.

They followed the wide ledge along the side of the cliff till they came to a small valley cut into the hillside, a valley that was thick with weeds and tangled grasses, and he turned to signal to her: Wait here.

The girl dropped to her haunches under a bush and sat there waiting while her father ran lithely to the head of the valley and around the other side. The slope was much steeper there, and when he slithered down back to her he put his mouth close to her ear and whispered, "She is still in the bushes here; there are no tracks out of this little valley." When the girl stared at him, wide-eyed and excited, he said, "It is moving very, very slowly, limping on three feet. I think it is badly hurt. I think it will be very easy for a strong man to catch it."

The girl looked around helplessly. "The vines . . . where will we find vines here for the net?"

He shook his head. "I do not know." It was an admission he did not like to make, and he scratched his head and grinned at her, letting her know his little weakness, and he whispered, "Never mind; first we will look again; we will see where the animal is."

He went silently into the thicket, parting the tall grass with the end of his bow, an arrow ready in case of trouble, moving slowly, one careful step at a time. The girl was behind him, her heart beating so fast that when he turned to smile encouragement at her he could see the fluttering on her chest. And soon he pulled up short and looked at the ground ahead of him and said, his voice tinged with disappointment, "The animal is dead."

She stood half behind him, staring over his shoulder at the silent, still body of the jaguar.

Bichu lay there, unmoving, her eyes closed; there was not a movement, not even of the furry belly.

They looked at the pool of dried blood by her mouth, wondering what had happened; and then the Indian reached out with his bow, prodded the limp body, and said marveling, "No, she is still alive." He stepped back quickly and turned and grinned at his daughter and said, "You see? I decided that I would catch this animal, and it has been made easy for me."

But the girl was staring at the jaguar, awed by the blood and the terrible hole in the sleek shoulder, with the flies buzzing at it, and the closed eyes and half-open mouth where the dark blood had caked. She thought that this was the most beautiful animal she had even seen and that someone had tried to kill it. She did not know why, but she felt great sadness. Since she had been two years old, she had never cried; but now there were tears in her eyes, tears that she was half-ashamed of.

She said softly, *"O pobre bicho,* the poor creature." In her heavy Indian accent it sounded like *"U pobru bichu."*

Her father was stripping off the long rope which he carried wound around his waist, and he touched Bichu again with the bow. When he was sure that she was quite unconscious he cut three short lengths of it with his knife, one for the forelegs, one for the hindlegs, and the third to tie around her neck so that he could drag her safely at the end of his rope, just in case she should recover enough to challenge his authority over her. With another man, he would have tied her to a pole and slung her across their shoulders, but his daughter (he thought) was too frail and delicate. When she made a move to help him, he said sharply, "No! Stand away! If it recovers . . ."

He knotted the shortest of the cords around Bichu's throat like a collar, and as he took hold of her forelegs and began to wrap the rope around them, Bichu suddenly awoke; she could smell the fearful alien scent of the Indian, feel his alien touch; and like an uncoiling spring she lashed out blindly with her three good legs, slashing instinctively for the throat with her foreleg and using the powerful hind muscles to thrust herself away from the ground.

The Indian fell backward, blood coursing out of a deep gash on his bare chest, and the girl screamed and dropped to the ground, covering herself with the blanket her father had told her to carry. And when in the silence she peeked out again fearfully, Bichu was gone.

Her father, shaken, was staggering to his feet, rubbing a bloodied hand over his chest; and she stared at him and began to cry, and he said bravely, "It is nothing, a small cut . . ."

There were four parallel slashes that coursed from his shoulder right down to his loincloth, bleeding heavily, and he stared at them somberly for a while; they did not hurt him very much. He said to the girl, "We will go back to where the fire is, and we will take the ashes and rub them into my wounds, and they will be well again. It is nothing."

She was ashamed of her hiding. She nodded and looked off to where Bichu had gone. She turned back to him, and to her astonishment her father was laughing. His tiny black eyes were wrinkled up, and he was laughing so much that the sweat was pouring off his face. He pointed to the wounds on his chest and said, spluttering, "We will tell them in the village how I was attacked by a large jaguar, how I beat it off with my spear, and how it ran from me in terror." He said again, slapping his leg, "We will go back to the fire and find some ashes."

She nodded. "And then?"

He scratched his head, leaving a bloody mark on his forehead, and thought for a while. At last he said gravely, "Then, we will go down to the river and begin counting the trees."

Like the shooting, the catching had been a casual thought; and now the thought was gone. There were more important things to think about.

As they walked away together, her father laughing again at his secret joke, the girl looked back once to where Bichu had gone; her childish heart was very heavy.

chapter four

Bichu could go no farther.

In the first burst of terror, when she felt the frightening touch of hands on her body, there had been only one thought, to get as far away as possible. She'd move as fast as her crippled limbs would carry her, quite heedless of the pain now because the danger was greater than the pain, and there was a driving reserve of power that pushed her to extremes of stamina.

She did not look back, and for the first time she was able to force away from her the consciousness of the blood that was coming from her mouth as she streaked through the bushes, ignoring the dark cavities under trees or rocks, or the secret recesses of the gullies and thornbushes where she might have hidden, because they were too close at hand and the touching hands, she knew, would follow her, seeking again to destroy her.

And not until she had raced away, heart pounding, out of the range of the alien scent, did she stop to turn and sniff the air, sniff it to assure herself that it had, indeed, been left behind her. She forced herself to listen, to explore with her eyes, to still the rapid rising and falling of the soft cream-colored fur on her belly; and then she fell to the ground and lay on her side, panting, whimpering, and suffering.

For a long time she lay there, instinctively trying to pull herself wearily, each movement hurting her, under the shade of the low-slung bushes, forcing a way in among them and curling her body up to take on the shadows that were all around her.

She lay for a long while, and then she found a tree with a sloping, gnarled trunk that reached up high above her and was easy to climb, and she limped heavily up it, turning at every step to peer through the foliage for any signs of pursuit. She could go no farther, and yet, there was the desperate need to hide deep among the friendly leaves and branches. She was conscious of the sound of her own breathing as she moved, and she tried to stifle it. There was a trailing rope around her neck, and it snagged on a twig, and when she pulled hard at it and the twig snapped noisily, she froze for a long time; even the movement of her belly stopped, until she was sure that the sound had brought no added danger to her.

She lay along a high branch and tried to scratch at the rope with her good leg, tried to tear it away with sharp claws, tried to strain her teeth toward it to bite at it. It was chafing her neck, and worse, it still bore the frightful scent that meant so much peril to her; it was a reminder of the Indian, almost as if he himself were still close beside her.

Her fury mounted as she struggled with it, and at last, close to exhaustion with the pain and the frustration, she gave up. She would not accept it, but neither could she any longer fight it. She lay on her side, the side that hurt her least, with one rear leg firmly anchored with deep-biting claws, and she slept, restlessly.

The sun rose higher, and instinctively, even in half-sleep, she moved her body to keep the cinnamon sunlight spread over it, using the camouflage as she had been taught so long ago. And then, suddenly, she awoke to full alertness.

Far away, in the midday silence when most of the animals were asleep and only the foolish birds were squawking, she heard the sound of alarm.

First it was the eerie cry of a day-sleeping *douroucouli,* the tiny night-prowling monkey that had to hide in the shadows of the daylight hours because of its overly sensitive eyes. Bichu knew that somewhere in the distance among the thick green branches the inquisitive stripe-faced animal was peering fearfully out of its hollow tree trunk at whatever it was that had arrested its attention; it was the first of the danger signals.

Then the sound rose to a crescendo as a dozen howler monkeys took up the cry; she knew that they would be angrily plucking at their long beards as they scampered up to higher points of safety among the tall trees, looking back as they swung easily from branch to higher branch, howling at a threatening presence. A flight of birds, then, flipping noisily through the foliage; and then the rustling of a porcupine's quills, much nearer. . . .

Nearer? Why, then, had she not heard the approach of whatever it was that was causing the disturbance? Why had she, too, not heard what the monkeys had heard or seen? Whatever it was, it was approaching silently; and a conscious effort at silence, as she herself was silent when she was stalking; was always a threat that meant death under crushing teeth or ripping claws.

She kept quite still and listened, and there was nothing to hear other than the usual forest noises. She turned her head very slowly and sniffed the air; there was no foreign scent either. She turned her body very, very slowly, so that her back was to the touch of the breeze, knowing that from this direction, where the scent would be carried away from her, the danger was moving in.

There was a shrill chatter from a parrot, a cry close by; it was coming closer, then. She was terrified that she could not smell or hear the source of the danger, and the terror sharpened her wits; it honed her instinct for survival. There was only one predator that could move so stealthily, so silently, so unobtrusively; she knew that the Indian was close by.

She heard the faint sound of blood dripping, and it was her own. It fell in tiny spots to the earth beneath her, trickling from the corner of her mouth. She swallowed hard and moved swiftly and silently farther up the tree, deeper into the enclosing blanket of the foliage.

And then she heard the whispering voices.

Urubelava had long ago given up hope of ever seeing again the fierce animal he had almost captured.

He had moved steadily on, with his young daughter, along the river's edge where the para trees were, fingering his piece of susu bark and wondering how many pieces of iron he would receive for his work.

And then, unexpectedly, he had pulled up short to stare at the sun-baked mud that was whipped up into tiny pinnacles and bloodied. He crouched down on his heels and fingered the mud delicately. And then, saying nothing while his daughter patiently waited for him to speak, he walked over to where the pile of rotting leaves was and looked back once more at the tracks in the mud, and up at the trees, and over to the other side of the river, narrow here and moving sluggishly. He kicked moodily at the broken shells, and he fingered the long marks on his chest where the savage animal that his daughter, surprisingly, had called the *pobru bichu* had slashed at him so viciously. . . . He squinted at the sun and then he raised a didactic finger and said to her slowly. "There was a fight. The animal fought here with a crocodile; it is just as I said." He was very pleased with the delight that showed on his daughter's face, that her father had so skillfully deduced the reasons for the blood up there on the bluff.

He pointed to the shells and said, "The animal came here to break open the nest and feed on the eggs. And somewhere close by, over there, the crocodile was waiting. And the crocodile attacked the animal, and that is why there is blood." He thought for a long time, then, and said at last, "We will follow the animal's trail, and when we catch up with it, I will kill it for the skin." It was a decision he could arrive at only with a great deal of thought, because he knew that this time, having said it, he must not fail, or his daughter would lose her respect for him. And this was something he could not bear to think about. So he said clearly, "It was a mistake to try to catch so big an animal alive; only with small animals. This time I will kill it for the skin. This is my decision."

She could not fully understand why she should not share his excitement, his pleasure; there was a sadness gnawing at her mind. She said to her father hesitantly, "But the trees, the para trees to be counted?"

He gestured broadly. "The para trees will still be there when we have finished with the skin. The trees will not run from us." He thought he had made a very funny joke, and he laughed and said again. "Only the animal will run from me; the trees will stay where they are, waiting for me to count them. They will not run; they do not know how to run." His tiny, porcine eyes were screwed up with his laughter.

But as they moved off together, she said, pleading, "Perhaps, if I find vines for you, you can make a net and capture it?" He shook his head, indicating the ash-covered gashes on his chest; the blood had caked in the ashes, making a great purple mess right down to his waist. He was afraid, but he did not want her to know.

He said, "A man cannot be hurt twice by a jaguar, because the second time, the jaguar will kill him. And if the animal kills me, what will you do then, daughter?" He was casting around for more signs in the mud. and he whispered happily, "This is a propitious month for me. First the money from the para trees, and then the money from the. skin. We will be rich. Over here."

He pointed, and as she followed him he turned to her and said very quietly, "I do not think it will be far. We will make no noise." It was all he needed to tell her; there was not a sound of any sort from them as they slipped like animals, crouched, through the denseness of the greenery. Once he stopped and signaled to her, pointing out the tracks of a vulture that had dropped down from the branches to gobble up some blood-soaked leaves; she nodded, saying nothing; her heart was very heavy.

He could not know it, but the blood had stopped dripping now.

High on a branch, far from where they stood, Bichu was drawing herself in deeper among the branches, sliding with infinite care over the rough bark. She was still listening to the danger signs. Her sharp eyes had caught a movement in a high tree far away from her, in the danger direction; a spider monkey was up there, staring down below; there, then . . . She waited.

Soon she heard faint sounds that should not have been there. She looked around her, examining every shadow, every splotch of filtered light that fell across her body; her camouflage was complete; all she could do now was wait. She kept still. Her round, solid head had dropped an inch or two, and her muzzle was pressed down to the branch. It was as if she were part of the great tree, a dappled shadow lying along it as silent and as motionless as a long-dead fungus sprouting from the coarse bark. She was part of the forest, and the forest was part of her; and nothing moved except her watchful, expectant eyes.

Soon she saw them. They were moving with care, the man in front and the girl behind him, taking one step and waiting, then taking another and waiting again. Then they were gone again, hidden by the bushes. But now she could scent them, and it was the same scent that was still on the piece of ragged rope that hung around her neck.

She caught another movement, which was nothing more than a glimpse of a lithe brown figure with the momentary sun on it, and another shadow close behind it; and then the closing forest hid them once more. For a long, long time nothing happened; and she knew that they had lost her tracks and were searching for them, not moving, but twisting their heads from one side to another, looking for telltale scratches on the tree trunks, or flattened blades of long grass, or yellow-green depressions in the moss.

And then they were right below her, standing there helplessly and looking around them, wondering. And she looked down at them. This was the moment for attack, the moment to put an end once and for all to the deadly pursuit. The old fighting instincts, all the teachings of her heritage, told her that this was the moment. A quick, easy bound to the green moss below her, with the sun and the brightness behind her, then a leap at the throat, a quick slash with the killing legs, a twist and a bound at the other ... It was all quite clear to her, the geometric precision of the movement ready in her mind, automatically, with no planning other than the overall pattern of instinct. She saw the whole pattern of the assault, without any thought or reflection, a pattern that had been outlined for her hundreds of thousands of years ago in the genes of her ancestors and was now ready to be brought to fruition in the perfection of her own smooth muscles and her speed and cunning.

She began, very slowly, to bring her long rear legs under her, easing them along the bark, listening for the slightest sound the movement would cause and knowing that there was none. She shifted her shoulder a trifle, moved her head up a fraction. And then the pain began to course through her body again, and she remembered the leap across the water where the crocodile had been, remembered the moments of unconsciousness. It was a warning. And in the instant of indecision, the two intruders moved on again, and the instant had gone.

Soon they were far away, still moving silently through the

bushes; and Bichu watched them until the leaves and the branches closed in behind them. And then, for a long, long time, she still heard them, the picture of them firm in her mind, the scent of them brought to her now on the breeze; it was a comfort to her that the scent of them was there, dwindling away but still strong enough to place with marvelous accuracy.

For a long time she did not move her body; only her head sneaked from side to side in short little glances. And then, at last, she began to back off toward the trunk of the tree, knowing that she should not twist herself around too hard or too far. Her leg hung uselessly, and once she stumbled and nearly fell, but she saved herself by driving the claws of her rear feet deep into the wood, tearing away a long hunk of bark. She whimpered once with the pain but then was conscious of a returning power in her shoulder; not much now, but the slightest feeling that if she willed it to move, it would. It was stiff and painful, but it seemed to her that it was regaining at least some of the lost strength.

Her rib cage was hurting her, and when she tried to twist her body, groping for a surer footing, she could hear the distinct grating sound of broken bone ends and feel with them the shooting agony that sped its way through her body. But she sensed that she was stronger at this moment than she had been since the bullet first had smacked so brutally into her.

She bit at her tongue and swung her body around to begin the descent, brushing aside the leaves and the twigs and the smaller branches. For a moment she stood there, stretching her long, smooth body and raising her head. Her hurt leg was curled slightly under the soft velvet folds of the fur on her chest, her head twisted a little to one side.

The colors in the sun and the shade were cream and brown, and yellow and black, and a rich, sleek, and glossy auburn. All the elegance and splendor of the forest seemed, at this moment, to be reflected in the dignity of her bearing; and if a man could have seen her now, he would have thought that nothing in the world, surely, could be more beautiful.

And then, as she began to move slowly down, there was a choking pain in her throat, and she snarled as the rope around it bit suddenly into her. She slashed out instinctively at this new unknown enemy. She tugged herself savagely away from it, her lips drawn back, her eyes on fire, her whole body twisting and turning and struggling. And then she fell.

The noose tightened around her neck and she hung there, slowly swinging from side to side, her forelegs (even the wounded one now) reaching out and pawing the air. The darkness began to sweep over her, a darkness in which great clouds of red were burning, in which the greens of the forest were nebulously misting and merging, getting darker and darker, with flashes of brightness coming and going, and great lights bursting, and over everything the pounding, frightening red that was slowly changing to gray and then to black.

One paw was hooked around the strangling rope as she hung there, turning gently like a carcass swinging on its hook; and then the coma came and took her completely in its shroud.

chapter five

When the sun began to sink, the forest began its evening cacophony. The silence of the afternoon receded, and with the general awakening it seemed as though the jungle were teeming with a hidden, mysterious life that had never been there before, a life that announced itself from a hundred thousand throats.

The parrots began their squawking first, crying out to each other loudly in the angry, raucous sounds that were meant as a warning to others of their species to keep away, well away, from the chosen territorial sites. A bird would settle in a tree, and its cries would announce to its neighbors: *This is my place, these branches belong to me, and no other bird shall come near them.* There were millions upon millions of other branches, just the same as these; nonetheless, the birds would cry: *Keep away, they are mine, and not to be shared.*

The claim to the territory would last for the whole night, and sometimes for night after night, and any intruder would be scared away by an angry fluttering of wings, a threatening ruffle of feathers, or sometimes by a quick, violent sortie with vicious beaks and predatory claws. The smaller birds would group together in colonies, with always a watchful male up on the highest branch of the little area that was theirs, and the females watching for grubs and crawling insects to feed their young.

Then the monkeys, a hundred different varieties of them, would leap excitedly among the treetops, watching for their enemies, clutching at succulent shoots as they swung past them, tearing at the choicest of the young leaves and nibbling away as they swung through the branches, their eyes alert and watchful. There was the tiny yellow tamarin, no more than five inches long, the marmoset that some people called the lion monkey because of its furry mane and leonine expression; it would scuttle its way through the fragile foliage, squeaking its anger at its neighbors, a furry handful of beauty and bad temper. The peccaries grunted as they rooted in the earth for grubs and roots, and the ugly tapir would whinny like a horse as he forced his way through the jungle in his constant search for the palm nuts that were his food, making his own path and not following the beaten animal tracks as the other creatures did.

The roar of the forest would become deafening at night, so loud and constant that sometimes a man would have to shout to make himself heard; it was all part of the hugeness of this great river basin. Some of the minor, nameless tributaries (only the larger ones, and there were more than eleven hundred of them, had been named) were so wide that a man could not see across them, and there were islands hundreds of miles across floating on the waters and breaking up in the rains; the water would rise as much as sixty feet in one night and drown any living thing that did not hurry to safety on the higher ground.

There was so much of land and of water and of forest; the great basin was a giant, and its sound was the sound of a giant.

The white herons, thousands of them, would wheel over the waters, adding their shrieking to the din; and when they settled and were silent, the predators of the forest would begin their challenging roars, so that there was never any true silence from the animals. Only when the monthly tidal wave, the dreaded *pororoca,* would sweep upstream at more that fifty miles an hour, twenty feet high and un-counted miles across, destroying everything in its path, then, over its thunder, from the animals nothing could be heard.

At night the little monkeys were silent, but the howlers would begin, and the predators, so that there was always a day sound and a night sound; and over all was the con-stant sound of the birds and the roar of distant waters.

With the sinking of the sun came the cold; after the steaming heat of the day, it was a relief. But from the noise, there was no escape.

All afternoon the Indian had been backtracking. When he had known, at last, that he had lost the jaguar's trail, he calmly lit a fire and squatted on the ground to stare into the flames while his daughter sat close by. She did not dare to speak to him; she knew what he was thinking; he was not called Urubelava, the stubborn man, for nothing.

He plucked idly at the matted wood ash on his chest, and she drew geometric patterns in the ground beside her,

waiting, tracing the patterns with a small stick. She bit at
the end of the stick until it was frayed like a brush, and
then she began methodically to rub the end up and down
on her teeth, cleaning them and whiling away the time.

He said at last, not looking at her, "Back there by the
canela trees, that is where I went wrong. The animal is
heading for the high country, but she knows that I am behind her, and so, she is turning away from the mountains,
thinking to mislead me."

It was a decision, and she was on her feet already, standing there with the twig in her mouth and smiling gently.
She asked, "The para trees?"

He shrugged. "They can wait. We will go back."

They walked together back the way they had come; but
now he was moving in zigzag patterns, a hundred paces
or so to one side, and then to the other, cutting his way
without much difficulty with his *facao* when there were
vines or bushes in his way. His bare feet made no sound
on the moss.

The sun was low on the horizon, and here among the
trees there were only slanting yellow rays that cast strange
shadows about them. The girl shuddered once, and he
looked at her and said, "There is nothing to fear."

He knew that she was afraid of the night, and when they
came to a huge ceiba tree, more than a hundred feet high
and fifty feet or more across its divided trunks, he said,
"Here; we will wait out the night here." There were brilliant orchids splashing the gray slab walls of its trunks, and
a delicate vine was threading its pale-green way up into
the high branches; and someone, many years ago, had
thrown heavy logs from trunk to trunk to make a rude
shelter. There were even stones left there from a long-ago
fire, and he was delighted with the unexpected find; a

house ready-built in which to spend the night, with smoldering embers at the entrance to keep out the animals and the spirits.

She was looking at the stones and he saw her trepidation and said gently, "It is not the *desatitos* who built their fires here. These were placed by our own people, the Arasuyas." There was always the fear of the river raiders; but they never left their firestones behind them, because they did not like the other tribes, their quarry, to know just where they had been. The Indian said, "Go, find me some wood to make fire."

In a little while she came back with a stick of *capirona* and a thick piece of broken and dried bamboo. He sharpened the stick with his *facao* and slipped his bowstring around it, and when he had twirled it awhile the bamboo began to smolder and the girl threw some dry grass over it; and soon it burst into flames and they both began piling on small slivers of wood until the flames were high. It was dark now, and he laughed suddenly and said, "Now it is dark, and I did not hunt for food."

She shrugged. "We have eaten. It was enough." Her father nodded. He curled himself up in his blanket, tucking his arrows in with him to keep the dew off them, and he was fast asleep before she had even covered herself up and lain down close beside him.

Once, twice, three times he woke in the night to feed more wood to the fire, and the last time he crouched over it for a while to drive out the bitter cold, and then he lay down and slept again.

The night-dampened rope was still stretching.

The Indian had made it a long time ago by weaving strands of flax together, twisting and binding, wetting down the strands and rubbing them with beeswax, testing the strength of it every so often by gripping it with his splayed toes and tugging at it with tough but delicate fingers. When he had finished it, he had slipped it around the bole of a tree and had pulled hard, repairing it again where it broke; it had taken him three days to make.

But that was a long time ago. Now the rope was frayed, and some of the wax had been eaten away by insects. And where the wax had gone, the dew was softening and stretching it; and where the stretching was, there was the weakness too.

But as the coma came and went, and came again and then left her wide awake and terrified with her immobility, Bichu could only know that it was cutting into the side of her neck viciously, like a living thing; its clumsy knot was rubbing raw the flesh at the side of her mouth, and when she snapped at it her sharp teeth closed over the knot and bit into it, deeply.

All through the night, in spasms of consciousness, she had gnawed away at it, getting the waxed threads into the side of her mouth and using her strong teeth on them. She chewed while she was conscious, and when the consciousness left her, each time the rope was weaker; it was a relentless, instinctive movement toward a sense of self-preservation that was intuitive and quite independent of reason. Her mouth and her tongue were lacerated with the effort. But the pain was so much a part of her now that she was barely aware of it; the stoicism of the wild animal was asserting itself.

The sound of her breathing was appalling, a strident, rasping sound. And when the blackness came, from time to time, she swung gently at the end of the rope until it went again and the light of the dawn seemed to come slowly to her, flared with reds and greens and yellows.

Soon the knot was firmly under her molars. She bit hard and deep, each movement of her jaws forcing the rope into its cut on the side of her lip. The insects, the ugly *carapatos* ticks and the *pium* flies that heralded the arrival of the day, were already filling their stomachs with the fresh blood that was around her muzzle.

A long brown anaconda, black-spotted and white-bellied, slithered along the branch over her head and watched her for a while. She was conscious that it was gauging her size and her helplessness, and she tried to snarl at it, pawing the air. The snake wound itself slowly and carefully around her as she struggled, and used her to slither to the ground, falling with a plop into the pool of water it was searching for. Through the wet mud it slid, looking for deeper water and for food; and soon she heard the shriek of a bitten peccary and knew that the snake had found its meal. There was a momentary silence, as though the creatures of the forest, the forest itself, knew that for the brief moment of death all sound must stop; and then the sound began to swell again and the deafening roar continued.

The sound was augmented now by a strange buzzing in her brain, and she twisted around, slashing at the rope with her claws in helpless savagery; abruptly the rope snapped, and she fell to the ground with a heart-stopping thud, splashing into the wet earth and immediately racing off to

one side in an instinctive drive for the dark shadows and
the cool of the moss. The pain was insupportable, but the
fear was greater; and when she fell at last, rolling over onto
her side and gasping, she knew that she was free again and
that the danger was gone. There was no thought of whether
or not this respite would last. There were strands of rope
in her mouth, and furiously she spat them out, hating the
scent of them. And then she gathered her strength together
and began to run.

The sun came up on her right, and the occasional bursts
of sunlight in the depths of darkness under the trees were
a comfort to her after the fears of the night. She was running from her own fear of the inexplicable; but soon her
courage came back with the soothing satisfactions of the
jungle, and her pace began to slacken.

She was running more easily now, not fast, but easier
than before, with one leg looped up under her body, hobbling along as fast as she could but still keeping the reserve
of strength for when she should need it; her instincts and
all the lessons she had ever learned were serving her well,
and one law was: *Always hold back and keep a reserve of
speed.*

And soon that burst of speed was needed. A small
groundhog was drinking at the edge of the river, one of the
thousands of rivers, and she was on it with a flash of fury
before it was aware of her presence, the sharp teeth crushing the ugly skull and the claws ripping out the dirty-gray
stomach. She crouched over it and filled her belly, and
when she was satisfied, she raced on again, trying to lose
the scent that was still with her: she could not realize that
it came from the marks of the cord at her throat, a rope that
had gone except in the scent it had left behind.

For a while she hid to rest in the hollowed-out stump of

a fallen tree, regaining her strength before she was completely exhausted. And when she ran on again, heading for the high mountains but moving in wide sweeps to confuse whatever enemies were behind her, she stopped once in alertness to stiff out the scent that was once more on the ground here; they had passed this way; for a while she followed the scent of the tracks; they were fresh. She looked around carefully and listened, and tested the wind, and separated the sounds she knew from the sounds that were strange. There was no fear now. But her watchfulness was great.

She gauged the infinite differences in the strengths of the scents, sniffing the ground and then looking carefully around her, moving on a trifle and then sniffing and searching again. She drank some water from a pool and then crept on, always to where the scents were stronger, moving with her old accustomed skill now, secure in the knowledge of her cunning. And in a little while she could taste the scent of burning wood. Her belly was low on the ground, part of the moss itself, as she crept toward the smell.

Under a cluster of wet ferns, over a fallen cinnamon trunk, through a tangle of vines, around a patch of drying-out bamboo ... Up into a small tree and down again, gently through a stream of sluggish water, up over the muddied grasses ... Soon she saw the fire. It was tiny, a few embers burning in the early dawn. And over it, the Indian was crouched.

For a little while, holding her breath, she watched him. And then she began to move back, with meticulous precision, into the cover of the foliage. She knew exactly where she had to go—a small cave she had passed, where she had paused for a careful investigation. It was long and narrow, almost too small to permit the passage of her body. And at the end of a long and tortuous tunnel, there was another way out.

She moved into the cave, squeezing herself in, and swung her body carefully around to watch, and to listen, and to wait.

Urubelava was carefully unwrapping the binding around one of his arrowheads.

The sharp fishbone had broken its point in the last evening's struggle through the bush, and on one of the other arrows, the one that had an iron point, the shaft had become warped in the damp beyond any hope of straightening. So now, very carefully, he was putting the iron head onto the good shaft and thinking about the iron they would give him for counting the para trees. He knew that he ought, at this very moment, to be counting them already and earning the good things he had been promised, and thinking about this, he said aloud, "But first, the animal, the *onca,* the jaguar." As though explaining away his guilt, he said, "I will not allow an animal to defeat me. It is a question of dignity."

His daughter was scraping dried blood off the crest of the harpy eagle, using a handful of earth to do this, before putting it carefully back in her black hair. The bundles were ready, all tied in string, and all she was waiting for was for her father to finish his morning drink. She said, a little petulantly, "I am hungry."

He shrugged. "We will find food." He stood up and cut some short, thick twigs and found a stone to use to drive them into the soft flesh of the ceiba tree for making a ladder that would take him up the great gray slab walls of its bark and onto the huge platform of its lower branches.

When he had climbed up there, he looked around and sighed when he saw, as he should have known, that there was nothing to see, even from up here, because the forest was too tightly packed around him. He jumped lightly down to the ground and gathered up his weapons and said, "This way. We will move toward the mountains, and we will look for the *onca*'s tracks." He spoke as though he were sure he would find them. True, it was easy enough to follow an animal over this soil that was wet nearly everywhere; but once a man lost the tracks he could search for days on end without finding them again; and he was worried that perhaps the animal had eluded him.

But, like most of the Arasuya Indians, he was a good tracker. And he was as persistent and as dogged as an animal himself. He said, explaining carefully so that his daughter should not think he was a fool, "If the animal knows that we are looking for it, then it will circle around to deceive us. Therefore, if we go first this way"—pointing— "and then"—pointing again—"that way, we will find its tracks. Except where the ground is hard, we will see them. And with my best arrow, I will kill the animal, and we shall have a fine skin to sell."

For a long time they moved together in wide arcs. The girl was feeling the hunger pains gnawing at her, but she said nothing, knowing that nothing would stop her father until he was sure that he was moving in the right direction for the challenge he had decided to accept.

At last he pulled up short and stared, and reached out quickly and snatched up a short length of broken rope, and said in astonishment, "This is my rope. . . ."

He dropped his weapons and crouched on his heels and

examined the rope, twisting it over and over in his hands. When he was quite sure, he said gravely, "The animal pulled at the rope that was around its neck, and bit it through." He stared for a while at the little pool of water there, and at the pad marks in the mud, and at the long thin line that meandered into the bushes, and he pointed and said idly, not much interested because it had nothing to do with the jaguar, "An anaconda, a small one." He got up and followed the pad marks along the edge of the pool, and he said, wondering, "Here, and here . . . four feet on the ground. And then three again. The animal is recovering."

The girl clapped her hands delightedly, and then her face fell as her father turned to frown at her. But he only said, "It is worthless to feel sorry for an animal. An animal is an animal." She nodded, pleased that he was not really angry with her.

The tracks were clear now; the *onca* had been running fast, not trying to hide its tracks. They led through a wide-open clearing where the sun was very hot—and where he nearly lost them again—and then into the darkness, where the vines were tangled so firmly in the high branches that they shut out all light from the sky. And again across a vast, open space where the insects buzzed and made him hurry to reach the semidarkness again, where the *mocuim,* the tiny bright-red acarus mites, could not easily survive in such enormous numbers; his skin was blotched and red and swollen with their itching when he reached the shadows again, and he smiled at his daughter, who was rubbing her skin frenziedly, and gave her a handful of powdered tobacco leaves, and said, "Chew this for us while I hunt."

He walked toward the sound of water, and when he came to the stream he stood on a rock and waited, and then sent

his best arrow slipping down into the shallows and brought
up a fat *corbina*, and walked back with the fish still on the
shaft and held it out for his daughter to take and cook for
them.

She was spitting out tobacco-colored saliva into her
cupped hands and rubbing the juice over her body where
the *mocuim* had raised the sore red rash, and he crouched
while she rubbed his back with it, and then stuck a stick
in the last pad mark he had seen, more as a gesture than
anything else; and then he made fire and they cooked the
fish and ate it, and they moved off together (leaving the
fire, as always, still burning brightly), following the tracks
until they lost them again.

He stood with his fists on his hips, glaring at the ground
as though it were consciously hiding its secrets from him,
and he said in a loud voice touched with anger, "We will
find them again. I have decided we will find them again."

And in the long, narrow cave, quite close by, Bichu heard
him.

The cave was little more than a deep crevice in a tall
slope of red mud, scarred with gray granite, that rose high
up to an ancient stone buttress. The stones had been hand-
cut, chipped with stone axes perhaps, and they were part
of an old ruin, buried deep in the jungle for uncounted
and forgotten generations; they were one of the mysteries
that would always give this unknown land a fascination
of its own.

It was said that no men, apart from the scattered Indians,
had ever been here; but half a millennium ago there were
stragglers, deserters, who had fallen out of the ranks of the
explorers who had once journeyed up the great river. Some
had survived and brought out tales of the warrior women
who had given the river its name. Once, the river had been

called the Orellana, after the noble captain who had first
tried to travel its length; and also the Mar Dulce, because,
though its waters were sweet, its width was so great that a
sailor could not tell whether he was on a sea or a river;
some even called it the Maranon, the Sea-or-Not, because
of its vastness. But once the surprising tales of the warrior
women had found their way back to Europe, the name
was firm in the minds of the romanticists of the era. It was
the Amazon, once and for all.

Some of those stragglers and deserters had found they
could live in the jungle; some had found themselves Indian
women and had become their slaves; some of them had
built homes and defenses against marauding tribes that
once lived here. And then they had died out, and the Indians had died out too, and all that was left were a few
scattered remnants of an alien culture, buried under lichen
and vine. Sometimes, when the rains pounded, great masses
of land would wash away, to become broken islands in the
delta, leaving huge red slashes of new earth; and here, all
that had long been buried would come to uncanny life for
a short time before the constant vegetation would bury it
once again.

And so, for a brief moment, there would be a reminder
that once there had been other life here that had tried to
tame the jungle and had failed.

The cave was a little way up from the bottom of the cliff
where the broken gray wall was, now beginning to disappear once more under the hungry vegetation. The roots of
an upended mangrove tree sprawled here, brought low by
the floods, and vines were thickly tangled in its outstretched, dying, ironwood limbs, stifling it, reaching out
with their tendrils and choking it as the roots strove like
giant fingers to find moist earth. The mangrove had already
lost the battle.

A mass of parasitic purple orchids was feeding on its rotting bark, and high in the dark trees above it, a flight of herons had settled in the branches of the taller trees that shielded them from the sun; there were more than a thousand of them, like blossoms in the trees; and soon, wary of the careless sounds made by the intruders, they took to their wings and wheeled away toward the river, toward one of the many rivers of the watershed.

Bichu watched them go, her bullet head tilted back and her eyes alert. It was part of the pattern of danger's approach. Crouched at the entrance to the cave, she was watching, listening, calculating. The cave behind her was a friendly refuge, dark and comforting; she had already explored it well. For the rest of the day she must stay here, stay here till the sun went down and brought the succor of darkness. The gray-brown walls inside were wet with seeping water, and strong-scented lichen was growing there. There were ancient bones in the wet earth, and broken rocks, and great slopes of granite that rose high up into the bowels of the mountain above her; and there was no other entrance.

She had found a *capybara,* a great rodent almost half her own size, four feet long and a hundred pounds in weight, a hundred pounds of solid muscle, and—for her—of sustaining food. It had eaten its fill of the succulent water grasses close by and was lying in the sun on its back, clicking away in its pleasure, and Bichu had killed it swiftly with one crunching bite; she had dragged it with her into the cave, provisioning herself for a sustained siege if necessary, knowing that with food and water she could stay here until her strength returned. She could not reason; but what man would do through logic, she, like all the animals, would do through the sound teaching of her own instinct. She had tucked the huge rodent deep into a broken cluster of boulders inside the cave against the time the hunger should come again, and had come back to the entrance to investigate the sounds that had caused the noisy herons to take flight. Her confidence was returning with her returning strength.

True, the pains in her body were still racking. But she had learned that she could tolerate them, although, from time to time, nausea swept over her, causing her to catch her breath and whimper.

She crouched in the mouth of the cave and looked out over the tops of the green-yellow banana trees, pressing her body tight against the earth, her claws gripping the soil, her long body tensed and ready for flight; the tip of her tail was twitching slightly. Far below, she could see the movements in the bushes.

She watched, more bold now, as the intruders approached. She could hear their careless voices, and when the wind changed briefly she could catch their scent. She took a last look around and moved deep into the recesses of the cave to wait for the darkness.

The sounds began to change again, growing to a deafening volume of shrieks and squawks, of howls and chatterings, with the splashing of the crocodile coming up from the waters below, and the sound, somewhere, of a distant waterfall. The wind began to whistle through the treetops, and the green broadswords of the banana leaves made a flat, rustling sound. The clouds gathered on the horizon, low in the night sky, dark and threatening. A hyena shrieked, screaming as it found the remains of another predator's meal, carrion that had been left to rot. There was the flapping of the giant night birds that swooped from the trees to catch scurrying rodents. The whole forest was at prey, as though nature's beauty was only for the daytime, to change with the darkness into a predatory demand for more and more sustenance, the death of one creature for the life of another. For millions of years it had been like this; it would always be so.

Bichu crouched at the edge of the cave. She had gorged herself on the *capybara*, and her stomach was full. She lay still and silent; only the twitching of the tail betrayed her awareness. She sniffed at the air, and she listened, remembering the disappearing sounds that had told her that the danger was going away.

She heard the noisy moaning of the howler monkeys, and the squawking of the parrakeets, and the harsh cry of a toucan close by—all the sounds that, to her, meant safety.

She crept forward a few paces, her body close to the ground.

The Indians had gone. She was safe again. She took a deep breath, gasping the cool night air deep into her lungs. Her proud head was up once more; her muscles were rippling again. Slowly, limping just a little, she stalked off, with great silent dignity, into the jungle that was hers.

chapter six

The bright-green land did not only stretch in every direction for all the miles a man could imagine; it also reared itself unbelievably high above his head.

The trees were so tall, their branches so high in the air, that a man cutting his way through the vines that were tangled in the rest of the greenery seemed no larger than an insect. Even the ferns which in other lands were ten, perhaps fifteen, feet high, here swayed their gigantic fronds so high above his head that he was an ant slowly winding his way among them.

There were leaves of every size and shade of green; long and narrow, or broad and expansive; thin as tissue or plumply fleshed out; bloated with pale-green sap, or delicate as gently waving lace. There were palm vines that twined themselves with incredible speed up toward the sun, and tendrils that reached out along the ground, fastening everywhere; and through it all would rear the ferns, their green tinged with a brilliant yellow. Between the wet moss below and the dark greens of the high branches were festoons of gaudy orchids, in purples, yellows, and startling reds, among which fronds of the ferns gently waved their long fingers.

The forest made a canopy so immense that a man could hardly comprehend it, and still, from time to time, the sun would break through it; and where the sun was, a million leaves and shoots and branches reached out and drank it in, fighting each other for survival, and all surviving.

But now the sky, where it could be seen, was darkening. The darkness came suddenly. One minute the sun was beating down, and the next minute there was shade and a sudden gray chill. . . . And then came the rain. The clouds swept in swiftly, and a moment later a sheet of water began to batter at the leaves. The sharp, clipping sound soon grew to a crescendo as the torrents of water poured straight down, pounding at the forest.

Within minutes there were new rushing rivers carving their quick way into the red earth of the mountains, and wet banks were collapsing to join the swelling flood in great muddy gouts, crashing into the water and momentarily forming small islands which soon were twisting over and over, upthrowing fingering roots, and swept away by the force of yet more water.

For Urubelava, at first, the force of the rain meant only one thing: the tracks he was following would be swiftly obliterated. For a moment he was impatient. But that was only for the first few minutes. The rains were a constant danger in his life, because they could change the contour of the land in a few hours, well-known trails could disappear, and hunting places could be swept away. And, worst of all, whole villages would be washed from their hillside perches, the fragile houses breaking up and collapsing to the ground, with the women and the children and the

monkey-pets all gone under a white-topped muddy maelstrom finding its way down to the sea. He remembered
well that only a few years before, soon after his new village
had been rebuilt after a fire that had swept the hillside, it
had been washed away; of the hundred and forty persons
living there, only thirty had been left alive.

So his first instinct now was to find a tree that was too
big to be overthrown by this sudden flood. The great ceiba
he first ran to, his daughter following swiftly, was too
shallow-rooted and would topple as soon as the river that
was carving its way at his feet undermined a mere foot or so
of the earth around its gigantic base. He ran on and found
a tall cedro, a hundred feet high and more than ten feet
across. The tangle of vines that for hundreds of years had
been feasting on it were so thick that he had to slice at them
with his *facao* to get near the trunk.

Father and daughter stood together then, their backs to
the heavy tree, and stared at the rain which pounded their
near-naked bodies and bounced off their glistening skins,
the water already forming rivulets at their feet. A bright-
red tree of balsam myrrh, splashed with purple orchids,
crashed close beside them; they could smell the strong scent
of its core.

The heat had gone, and the water was cold around their
knees, and Urubelava reached up and slashed at a vine
and threw it over one of the lower branches and swarmed
easily up it, squatting in a great gray fork and pulling
his daughter up after him; she was laughing. Below them a
river boiled in fury that was only half an hour old.

And now, a rare and beautiful phenomenon appeared.
Somewhere not far away, there was a break in the clouds,
while the rain still beat down noisily all around them,
hammering at the foliage with an incessant drumming

sound that was still growing in intensity. But where the slanting rays of the strong sun cut through the trees and the rain, the whole forest was suddenly turned to an iridescent yellow-gold, turned to purple as they watched, and then to gold again. The bright greens were suffused with the gold and then the red again, and the changing colors became gold-purple. There was a startling glow over the whole jungle, a glow that seemed like flames fighting the water. The uncanny phosphorescence was frightening in its intensity.

The girl, staring around her, began to tremble, and her father, who had seen this once before, smiled at her and raised a knowing hand and said, "It is a wet fire that covers the whole of the earth. It will not harm us."

The glow seemed to hang from the trees, and all the greens were now wiped out and replaced with burning gold, as though only this light could reveal a latent coloring in the trees, now shining in a glory that few men, surely, could ever have witnessed. The cold and motionless yet ever-changing fire was all around them; it was part of them; even their bodies shone with it.

The girl stared at it, and at her father, knowing that if he said it was harmless, then it was indeed so. She smiled when he said, "It is more beautiful than all the flowers of the forest, and it is not given to everyone to see it. I, myself, have seen it many times. Many, many times."

When he had been a child his father had told him what it was, and he had learned then not to fear something he could not really understand, even though it looked so very frightening, as though a wet flame were coming to devour everything in sight. But now he could feel his heart beating faster, because at that time there had been others in the village who knew that this was the manifestation of one

of their strange and angry gods. And indeed, a few days
after, three men in the village had been bitten by rats and
had died. So now, he was not too sure; just sure enough to
comfort the fears of his daughter.

The brilliant glow was yellow, and then red, and it
slowly changed once more to purple. And the purple did
not break out into gold anymore, but instead took on the
color of the rain, and the strange light was gone. Urubelava said, as though the going were his own doing, "You
see? It did not harm us."

Marina was looking down now, at the land on which
they had been standing just a little while before. The water
there was deep now, and rushing fast, and a python was
struggling in it. She saw the upturned, struggling legs of
another animal. Was it an antelope? The rain still pounded down.

Close by, there was a tearing sound, and then a slowly
growing roar as the giant ceiba they had left began to fall.
Great tangled vines held it for a moment, and it swayed
drunkenly from side to side, crashing into heavy branches
and shearing them off to thunder down into the new river.
And then it turned, gathering speed as it spun around,
and crashed with a mighty roar down to the ground. Over
the roar of the water and the thunder of the falling tree,
the birds shrieked, and the mingled sounds were deafening.

There was a gap in the darkness of the forest around
them now. The giant tree had torn out part of the back-
cloth, and far away beyond the hole in the wall of green
there was the sight of a mountain slope, bush-covered,
dark with the rain. Urubelava looked at it, and looked at
the fallen ceiba tree, and patted the branches they were
crouched in as though to reassure himself that this tree,

this deep-rooted cedar, would not also crash to the ground and kill them. He knew that the water was rising and that he must make up his mind quickly, but he did not want to hurry, because this was something he was not accustomed to. The indecision was almost more than he could bear, but he said at last, pointing, "We will go to the mountain there; it will be better."

The girl looked down at the water, and her face was frightened. But, having made up his mind, Urubelava was firm. He said, "The water is not deep. We can walk in it."

She nodded. He slipped first down the vine he had thrown up, dropping more slowly as he neared what was once ground, and finding that the water came only up to his waist. He looked up and grinned, and Marina came down after him, and he caught her to hold her against the strong flow of the water; it made little V-shaped waves as it divided around their bodies, and they slowly waded, feeling out each step, toward the mountain.

Once she slipped and disappeared under the water, and when he dragged her up she was gasping; but soon she began to laugh with the excitement of the adventure. It was something she could talk about for a long time when she got back to the village. She sobered suddenly, hoping that when she got back the village would still be there. There was no thought that she herself, and her father, might not return, even though she knew well that rain like this could, and did, easily kill.

A torn and broken tree came hurtling by them in the water, and for the first time Urubelava was worried; the water was deepening, getting faster as it swept down to join one of the many rivers that would all, in time, be part of the great Amazon itself. A dead vulture, skinny under

its wet brown feathers, was floating past them, and soon the water was only up to their knees as the ground seemed to rise up underneath them. It was trembling; they could feel it rocking under their feet.

The girl looked at her father in alarm, and she started to cry because she was aware of the fear on Urubelava's face. He grabbed her wrist and pulled at her, and shouted, "Quickly; we must move quickly now!"

The ground heaved under them, and the earth began to shudder, and when he lost his grip on her and floundered in suddenly deep water, she grabbed at the narrow trunk of a tree and screamed. It seemed that the whole world was rushing past her on the water. She saw a tangled mass of thorns rip at her father's flesh and drag him under the water as it toppled; and then, fighting them with his *facao* and his strong arms, he came to the surface again, slashing at the tendrils that had encircled his body and cutting himself loose from them as he struggled toward her.

She was conscious now that she was moving, the tree moving with her, still upright but slipping slowly down the side of an underwater hill. The movement was slow, and steady, and insistent, and it covered a large area.

All the land around them was moving, sliding, gathering speed, twenty, fifty, a hundred acres of it and more, a great wet island of tangled vines and shrubs and bushes and trees, all inextricably mingled and slowly breaking free from the rest of the earth. One of the trees nearby canted over and then fell, casting up its broken roots at a jagged angle against the sky, throwing up the wet mud with them.

It was no time for talk. Urubelava threw his arms around his daughter and dragged her, half walking, half swimming, looking back over his shoulder at the towering, tottering trees. One arm around her narrow waist, he struck out fast, pumping his legs like an animal. A great mound of earth thrust itself up beside them and broke away, and now the whole island righted itself and there was clean swirling water all around them, on both sides and behind; in front they could see nothing but tangled and shining vegetation, twisting and turning like the living thing it was. Another tree fell, a great flattop thorn, and he pulled her aside and said, "It is all right; the island is steady now; it will float."

The weight of her in his arms was heavy as the mud sucked at her, and as he pulled her free of it a great gray boulder went splashing past them, rolling down to the river; it was as big as any house that Urubelava had ever seen. They felt the island swinging around, and they could no longer see its borders, and it thumped heavily into the side of a cliff of red sandstone, the water coursing red down it, and was still. The dark body of a drowning animal was thrashing nearby; a piece of the island broke away and disappeared; and in the torrent that came out of nowhere two huge entangled trees were being tossed over and over like broken matchsticks. A tiny antelope was steadying itself on a log as it swirled past them, its huge eyes wide with fright, its ears lying back, its delicate legs balanced precariously; and as they watched, the log rolled over and the antelope went under the water; it thrashed about for a moment and then it was gone.

But now the island that had carried them was an island no more. It had wedged itself strongly against the wet earth of the mountain, and as it hung there, the ever-probing roots were already stretching out all around them to weave a skein that would hold the new land firmly to the old, until the rains should once more tear it. And over it all there was a strong, sweet smell of the wet forest.

The birds, a million of them, were wheeling and squawking, and for hundreds of miles all around them frightened animals were wrestling with one of their greatest, most constant enemies. Many of them would lose the battle.

The forest was being stirred, like a gigantic caldron of muddy, vine-laced earth, in which trees more than a hundred and fifty feet tall were twisting and writhing.

Every living thing in the great forest was fighting for its life against the rain.

Bichu was one of them.

The water was swirling around her, and she expanded her soft and lovely chest, its fur bedraggled, and laid her head back, not trying to swim yet but letting herself be carried with the water until its force should diminish enough to let her fight it.

It carried her down the mountainside she had so laboriously climbed, turning her over and over like a plaything of stuffed rags, and when she reached the bottom it was as though she had been swept down a waterfall in which the water was blood red with mud and green with uprooted vegetation. Once a log had thudded into her bruised body, and she had slashed at it instinctively; and a tangle of thorns on long, trailing branches had ripped at the soft skin of her belly, drawing blood. She had fought the trailing thorns for a long time, tangling herself in them and ripping her way free again, twisting over and over in the boiling water.

The water had become red, slimy mud that was sucking her in, and she struck out against it, thrusting the pains behind her. She found solid ground and began to drag herself on it, and then the ground became mud again as a wave of water swept over it, and a morass of intertwined branches caught her and flung her savagely back at the river; and again she was turning over in it, striving to keep her head above the water. The rain pounded down on her; it seemed as if there were as much water above the river level as below it.

She found a broken branch and clung to it; gripping it with her claws, and when the branch went under, caught in the strong current, she struck out for what seemed to be the shore, swimming strongly in spite of the blinding pain inside her; the pain had become bearable now, however terrible it might be. She was coughing blood again, but it meant nothing to her. The piece of land she was heading for slowly crumbled and broke up; and where there had been solid earth, there was only a tangle of falling trees, crashing into the water around her. A heavy branch fell across her back as she struggled to the surface again, driving her deep into the mud; she thrashed around to bring her head up, gasping for air and swallowing wet earth. The mud gathered her up and swept on; a twisted sapling had wound itself around her body like a rope, and a sharp twig ripped the skin from the back of her neck. She was moving fast with the mud, and she was almost oblivious of all the chaos around her; the coma was coming back when she most needed her strength.

And at this moment, she let the swirling jungle take her. She stopped fighting it. She closed her eyes and let herself drift into semiconsciousness.

All around her she could vaguely hear the shrieks of other animals; the *kinkajous*, clinging onto their own steel-strand tails; the coatis, routed out of their sleepy sloth by the rain; the ocelots, angry at being so rudely torn from their daytime lairs; the *cariucus*, marsh deer, armadillos,

antelopes, and *agoutis;* even the giant otters were squealing in fear and anger at the waters that were carrying them
far from their favored territories.

A tribe of *douroucoulis,* the night-traveling monkeys,
was calling out weird, pathetic cries, driven out of the
darkness they preferred by the rain and the turmoil around
them. An anaconda was swimming easily close beside her,
ignoring her in its mastery of the red water. A shattered
anthill was churning over and over close by, covered with
a boiling mass of white termites, millions of them. And the
rain went on and on, great sheets of solid water pouring
from an ever-lightening sky.

And when, at last, the rain stopped and the sun broke
through, the jungle was steaming, and its floor was chaotic.
There were mud-covered roots sticking up fifty feet into
the hot air like probing, mud-caked fingers; there were
great boulders split open by the force of the water; there
were gaping new holes in the sides of the mountains, and
red slices of shining sandstone where the green lichen had
been torn away. There were piles of lacy ferns, and thorns,
and broken branches, and uprooted trees, all higgledy-
piggledy in the fast-drying, steaming mud.

Soon the greenery would cover it all again, but now there
was nothing but molten earth and all the broken life that
once it bore.

When Bichu opened her eyes again, her body was stiff
with the dried mud caked to her flanks. Her hindquarters
were half-submerged, and she dragged herself wearily·out,.
shaking herself like a dog. The sun was hot on her back,
and she pulled herself under the shade of a fallen tree,
using the hollow of it as a refuge while she looked around
her at the newly changed jungle, sniffing the wind and finding a hateful scent on it that caused a shudder of fear

through her body. She crouched low, pressing deep into the earth, and she crawled toward the scent, hunting its exact location so that she might more easily avoid it.

The hair along the back of her neck was standing up as she smelled it. And then it disappeared as a breeze began to blow lightly; and then it was there again, stronger now, and she searched out the direction of the wind and moved to one side so that it was straight ahead of her. Her eyes were bright and shining, inquisitive and cautious at the same time, and she held her belly low on the ground, gliding over it in silence, moving in short, sharp runs from side to side.

She could smell burning wood now as the wind shifted. She was too close. She pulled back. Close by her there was a stand of wild sugarcane, heavily interlaced with *punya* vine, and she drew herself in among the sweet stalks.

She would wait here for a long, long time, before she would move, and would make very sure that it was safe to do so.

chapter seven

After the rains, the land was bright and clean and shining. It showed no signs of exhaustion; instead, it was refreshed and reinvigorated, and the tangled vegetation was already finding new roots, groping to bind the broken soil again. The animals were finding new lairs, and the birds were wheeling high as they sought out the old familiar places.

There was the stench of death everywhere, for many of the animals had died; but their death was part of the new life that was springing up all over the watershed. The steam rose up off the greenery and the red mud, and the sounds were less than they had been before. There were the cries of the birds as they settled back in the trees, and the gentle rill of running water, and it seemed that the whole land was at peace.

Urubelava said, not worrying about it too much, "I do not know where we are, daughter."

He lay on his back under the shade of an upended lupuna tree. The giant cupola of its top had crashed down onto a mossy bank, and its tight bundle of roots, too short for any stability in such a storm, were more than fifty paces away along the length of the trunk, half in and half out of the new river. Its dark, broken branches were like a huge fan spreading out from the wet earth, casting a vast semicircular shadow over the edge of the deep river.

The moss under his shoulders was wet and warm, and he twisted around and pointed and said, "There, where the mountain is, that is where we must go."

The girl was cleaning the caked mud out from between her toes, sitting cross-legged on the ground with her cloth around her waist and a bright-yellow flower in her hair; the red crest that her father had given her had been lost in the storm.

Not looking up at him, not thinking, she said, "But the para trees are down there, by the old river."

He nodded slowly. "Ah, the para trees." He got up and began to examine his bow carefully, looking for a warp in its tapering haft. He said, "I must find fat for the bow. Wait here. I will come soon."

She nodded, and when he had gone she got up and started collecting wood for a fire; it was hard to find anything that was not soaked through, but she found some broken branches of soft styrax wood that he could slice into slivers with his knife, and she broke off some of its twigs and laid them out in the sun to dry. She found a fallen pentaclethra which she knew would burn even when it was wet, and broke off some pieces and dragged them out into the sun too. And when her father came back, the fire was built and ready for him to light.

A man did not have to go very far in this jungle to hunt out his food, not if he could move silently like a hunting animal. There were a hundred different kinds of animals, and a thousand different kinds of fish, and birds without number; it was merely a matter of choice, of taste, of selection.

He was carrying a peccary he had killed, slung across his shoulders, and his bare red chest was shining with sweat that ran down to his waist, making little rivulets that soaked his loincloth. The scars were red, with the ash all washed away. He looked at the wood she had gathered and nodded and strung the peccary up on a root of the lupuna to skin it, letting the entrails drop into the water. He was careful to keep his feet away, because at the first handful of intestines, the water had been churned up by a darting shoal of black-spotted piranhas; it was easy enough to avoid them. He lit the fire with his sticks and his bowstring and then carved out a hunk of meat for his daughter to cook, and while he waited he carefully stripped off some of the peccary's fat and rubbed it slowly and carefully up and down the haft of his bow.

He waited for her to speak, sensing what she was thinking but she was busy tending the meal, turning the hunk of flesh over and over on the end of a stick; only when she came over to take his knife and cut it into two pieces did he look up at her and say, "The trees will come later. First I must find that animal, the *onca*, the jaguar, and I must kill it." He waited a little while for her to answer him, but she did not, and at last he scratched at his head and said, "It will not be easy, because there will be no tracks now. But after the rains, the *onca* will go to the river to find food among the animals that have been hurt, and when she moves, she will make fresh tracks, and that is when I will find her. This time she will not escape from me."

The girl was slowly slicing up the half-cooked meat. She

said, "A jaguar does not have to go to the river to hunt."

"This one does."

"Why is this one not like any other jaguar?"

"Because she is hurt. She cannot hunt for her food as easily as another jaguar, and she will die of starvation un-less she finds food that she can kill easily." There was a touch of triumph in his voice, and he took great pleasure in teaching his daughter. He said, "At the river, after the floods, there will be many animals that are dying, animals that have broken their legs or their backs and can no longer run even from a wounded *onca;* she will know this, and that is where she will look for food." He got up and ges-tured with his hands. He said, "I will say something else of value; she will find that it is still easy for her to catch fish, even though she cannot run down an antelope or a peccary; and the fish are in the river. When my bow is ready, I will make a raft, and we will go down the river and look for her. We will look for her tracks, and we will find them, and this time I will not lose them as I did be-fore."

It was a matter of pride. For a long time he had been silently ruminating, thinking what kind of a figure he must have cut for his daughter, a hunter who could not track even an *onca* that moved slowly, on three legs, and with blood dripping from its mouth whenever the effort to run became too strenuous. It was undignified to admit defeat; and to Urubelava, who had so little else, dignity was a matter of importance. He had almost forgotten about the money for the skin, because even a great deal of money was something that could disappear easily and leave noth-ing behind. But a man's character was a vital, honorable thing that had to be carefully guarded.

He took the meat from her and began to chew on it

with his sharply filed teeth, the hot fat running down over his chin as he sliced it at his mouth. He said, "It is necessary to think what an animal will do. That is why I am a good hunter, because I think what the animal will do."

Urubelava laughed easily, like most of the people of his tribe, and there was great amusement in him as he strode toward the river and raised his voice, shouting out loud into the forest, "*Onca!* Wherever you are, I will find you!"

For a long time he could not stop laughing.

But his daughter knew that he would find the tracks, and find the jaguar, and that he would kill it. Even the knowledge of the money the skin would bring could not lighten her heart.

Urubelava belched loudly, and he waved his knife at her and said, "Go and find me a balsa tree I can cut. We will make a raft now."

She walked into the forest, and Urubelava rubbed some of the fat once again into his bow to keep it supple, and then he lay down on his back and dozed for a while in the shade of the lupuna tree, letting his stomach digest the load of fresh meat and belching noisily once in a while. It was very pleasant to lie in the cool shade with moss under the shoulders and think about nothing at all.

But the girl was thinking of the jaguar. She could not drive away her sadness, nor could she understand it; as her father had said, it was foolish to feel for an unfeeling animal. And yet . . . when they had tried to rope it, it had seemed to her that when the *onca,* the jaguar she had thought of as *o pobru bichu,* had come out of its coma, it had been looking, momentarily, straight into her eyes. It had seemed that there had been a kind of empathy there. She knew that this was a foolish idea; and yet . . . The jaguar's eyes were huge, and dark brown, and long-lashed, and very beautiful, and in them there had been fear and great hurt; it did not bear thinking about.

She found a balsa tree with many long straight branches, and she wandered around looking for some *punya* vine, which she knew her father would want as well, seeking a tangle of it that he could easily cut with his sharp knife and use to bind the balsa logs together. She found some winding among a stand of wild sugar, and she made a small noise of pleasure, because sugar was rare here and her father would be pleased that she had found some sweet food for them.

She had no knife, so she tore at a stem with her strong teeth and bit a piece off and took it back to where Urube-lava was lying in the shade humming gently to himself, and she said, "I found balsa, and the *punya* vine you will need to tie the logs together. It is close by, over there."

He nodded. "Good. I did not tell you about the vine, I am pleased that you thought of it."

She brought her hands out from behind her back and showed him the sugarcane and said, "And look what else I found. Sugar."

He laughed delightedly, showing his surprise, and took the sugar stem from her and chewed on it happily, and he got up and said, hefting his *facao*, "Show me, daughter, I will cut more sugar first, and then I will cut vines, and then I will cut the logs, and soon we will have a fine raft to take us where we want to go."

She nodded and then asked, "And where is that?"

He shrugged. "We will ride with the water for a while. The big river is near here."

The big river was not the Amazon itself; it was one of the many, many tributaries that, by comparison, were no more than insignificant streams. The whole watershed was

a mass of these rivers, some new, some a hundred thousand
years old. Some of them broadened into swamps, and some
of them cut their way sharply through buried rocks. All
these thousands of rivers laced together, joining and re-
joining, and finding their way to the great Amazon itself,
which still, in these parts of the basin, was wild and untamed.

When they came to the sugar stand and the *punya,* he
gave her his knife to gather some canes, while he looked up
at the balsa tree and selected the logs he would cut. He would
not need many, not for just the two of them; four, perhaps
five, good straight logs would suffice. Now that the sun was
getting lower in the sky, he took his bearings, not thinking
much about it but idly figuring out where the little island
that had broken away with them had carried them. It was a
long way, but it did not matter very much. An Indian could
not get lost even in this immense jungle; all he had to do
was remember to keep the sun, where it broke through the
trees, in the corner of his shooting eye when he began his
day's march, and let it move slowly around to warm the
front of his face. Then, sooner or later, he would catch a
glimpse of the high mountain through the foliage, the
mountain that looked like a girl asleep, and he could move
toward her breast, and home was then not far away. And
behind him there would be the river, one of the many
rivers that would have, for him and for the other Indians,
its own particular characteristics to make it, however far
along its banks he might stray, easily recognizable. Sometimes it was the color of the water, or its speed, or its depth,
or the way a certain plant grew more lush on its banks;
or sometimes it was merely a matter of instinct.

Staring at the balsa wood he thought, a little guiltily,
about counting the para trees, which was what he had left

his village to do; but he put all thought of them firmly away from him, for after all, he had told his daughter: *First, we will catch the animal. . . .*

She brought him back his knife when she had wrapped a dozen sugarcanes in a piece of liana and slung them over her shoulder, and she stood by patiently while he hacked at the balsa wood, cutting five long poles and pointing their ends carefully the way his father had taught him. He crouched down and roped them firmly together with the *punya* and wondered whether he should put another stabilizing bar across the end of it. He decided not to. After all, the raft would be abandoned when it had served its purpose, left on the bank to rot, with all the other things that were being molded, with time, into the forest humus. Or perhaps, he thought, he would break it up and hide it, so that any passing *desatitos* would not know that one of the Arasuyas had passed this way.

He wondered about the *desatitos,* and spat into the moss under his feet.

Bichu had lain there a few hours ago, almost precisely where he was working.

She had been watching him while he was half-asleep in the shade nearby, watching his daughter as she moved into the forest to search for the tree. Indeed, the girl had passed quite close; and Bichu had drawn back into the cover of the canes. At one moment she wondered whether she should pounce and kill, because this was the scent of the danger that had pursued her for so long. But she also knew that the danger was twofold and that to attack only half would put her, weakened as she was, in a vulnerable position. And so she had watched, with just the tip of her tail moving slightly.

When the girl had started to bite into the sugarcane, releasing its sweet smell, Bichu had moved back slowly, her eyes always alert, until a dense screen of foliage masked her from the danger. And then she had begun to run, forcing her torn body into its rhythm, loping along quickly with one forefoot just lightly touching the ground, pushing herself hard because she must concentrate on speed and put this danger, which always seemed to be near her when she least expected it, once and for all far away from her. It was an instinct to force herself beyond the limits of her endurance, not so much out of fear as to avoid the danger that caused the fear; she would run as far as she could go, and then keep on running, driving herself along by the stubbornness of her will to stay alive. She would run until she dropped.

When the danger was a long way behind her, she stopped to rest, for the dizziness had come over her swiftly. She could not know how hard she was pushing herself. The pain of reopened wounds was terrible, but she knew now that the pain could be borne.

She dragged herself to her feet and stumbled on again, much more slowly now. She was not aware that her pace had slackened.

An antelope startled her when it came out of the bushes and fled at her scent; why had she not smelled it or heard it? And when she instinctively gave chase because she was hungry, the pain welled up inside her with explosive force; they had become so much a part of her life now that she had them thrust away from her consciousness; it was almost as if another bullet had smacked into her. The hunger was nothing, but the weariness and the pain were acute.

And now she was at last aware of the weakening; she had pushed herself beyond her limits. Even the determination of an animal to stay alive was more than a matter of willpower. However great that determination might be, there came a time when the muscles could not respond to the mind's command. Blindly, staggering and falling, Bichu limped toward a tree, the nearest solidly standing tree that was at hand, not pausing to scent out danger. She began to climb, slowly and mechanically, reaching up with one claw and trying to drive it deep into the bark and heave her long body up.

She felt the last of her strength failing. She snarled and drove her claws deeper into the branch; they would not hold; she fell.

Everything about her was dark. She was aware of nothing. The forest was sweetly scented, and alive, and clamorous around her; but she lay still; there was no consciousness at all. Once she shuddered and then lay still again.

High in the branches above her head the vultures were watching. It was a good time for them. The river and the swamps were full of helpless animals, some still living, some recently dead, some already beginning to decay after the midday heat. The vultures had already gorged themselves on carrion and were out looking for more, filling their filthy bellies with dead or still-living flesh, it did not matter which.

They were the big king vultures, with shiny white feathers on the body and black wings and tails; their featherless heads were gaudily and obscenely colored with scarlet and yellow and purple and blue, and their wingspans measured more than eight feet from tip to tip. Their sharp, steel-strong beaks could rip through a skull with one blow or delicately pick out a still-living eye with lightning

speed. Above them a flight of condors was circling, led by a
monstrous male that carried on its flattened head a dark,
purpled comb that was blackening with age; the bird was
more than twenty years old, with all the strength and cunning of its years. There were splashes of white on its black
wing feathers, and it flew, a little apart from the others, as
though asserting its superiority over every other feathered
creature; its appetite was voracious, and the blunted,
elongated center toe of its claw could rip out the throat of
a fully grown deer.

This condor had come down to the forest from the
high Andes, driven by an inexplicable animal urge. It had
joined hunting forces with others of its kind, and with the
king vultures, and for many years they had terrorized the
forests over which they flew. Even the Indians knew of
him, and many of them had tried to catch him, for the prestige of bringing so monstrous a bird captive to their village.

There was a set method of hunting the condors. The Indians would wait until they saw by the heavy flight of the
bird that its stomach was full; they would climb the highest
trees and watch, and when the condor settled on its mountain perch, where it would sleep like a dead man through
the heat of the day, they would take their ropes and would
climb, moving easily like mountain goats, and rope the
great bird whose sleep was as heavy as a coma. And they
would drag it—screaming when it awakened and found itself a captive—back down the steep mountain in a useless
triumph.

They would keep the bird captive, with a rope around its
leg, tied to a tree in the center of the village, where anyone who passed could pause to admire the courage of the
man who had caught it. And then sooner or later, it would
die, however much they fed it, and then these simple peo-

ple would be sad, because they loved their pets and could not understand why they should not continue to live together in harmony.

But on the wing, in their free state, these birds were greatly feared. And the big, aged male was more vicious than the rest of them. His stomach now was full, but the lethargy had not come to him; he was circling now, high above the others, and watching with them the motionless form of the jaguar lying so carelessly exposed in the grasses below. For in the world of the great condor, any animal that lay down and did not hide was a dying animal.

He saw that the gaudy king vultures were preparing to land in the high branches of the tree; later they would drop down one branch at a time, splashing the areas with bright color, approaching slowly as was their custom, dropping down a few feet and then waiting for any sign of life or danger, for this was an animal they would leave alone unless it had been weakened by age or sickness.

Then he swooped and dropped heavily straight to the ground, the white ruff at the base of his naked neck bristling. And then the king vultures, learning of the safety from him, dropped down to join him, each showing off his daring by approaching closer and closer to the animal. The giant condor strutted nearer, dragging his great wings, his darting neck searching out, his ugly head twisting and turning. He was peering greedily at Bichu's closed eye, calculating, expecting. In a little while, he moved around and stared at the other eye, flexing his long muscular neck for the lightning strike; the sharp beak was wet with saliva. One of the others, a female, came down to join him. She fluttered her feathers at him, showing that she was going in for the kill. But as soon as she moved forward he shot out his great head in a vicious rebuke. The female squawked and pranced away; and Bichu awoke.

She found a dozen of them, or more, swooping down from the branches above her, their heavy wings almost darkening the sky with their shadows, like the shadows of death.

Her awakening was instinctive. At one moment she was in a coma, not even scenting the foul stench of blood-soaked feathers or the carrion-coated breath. And in the next she was wide awake and fighting for her life, for these birds would tear out her eyes and rip out her living intestines, a danger only because there were so many of them and she herself was so weakened.

She was aware, too, and again it was an instinct, that only while she was dying would they dare to attack her. She forced herself to fight. She would not lie down and let them devour her. And sometimes life is a matter of willpower.

She snarled and shot out a claw—it was the bad one—in a sideswiping, lightning-fast motion that caught the great condor on its breastbone and sent it sprawling clumsily on the ground; and then, with a bound, ignoring the pain, she was in among them, the hunted turned hunter, striking out with tooth and claw, snapping and ripping. She held the great condor down with a heavy pad and ripped at its neck with her teeth. The others were rising now, screeching and croaking, flapping clumsily along the ground and working their giant wings until they were airborne. And then they wheeled high above her head and still peered down at her with their sharp, long-distance eyes.

The dead, ancient condor was still on its feet, its head torn off and its neck pumping blood. Its ten-foot wings were beating horribly, and Bichu spat and pounced upon it, then began relentlessly to tear it apart, stifling the hunger pains with its lean and leathery flesh.

This was a bird so immensely powerful that sometimes it would take a fully grown turtle out of the mud, carry it up a thousand feet or more, and drop it on hard rock to shatter its shell; then it would glide down at its leisure and tear apart the flesh with its cruel beak. Bichu could know little of these things, though she had seen them happen. But somewhere in that deep recess of the mind where heredity stores its secrets, she knew that this was an enemy.

After she had eaten, she lay down in the cool grass by the edge of a pool of clear, fresh water. And then she vomited and began to cough, but she found some *sudu* grasses and chewed on them to settle the pains in her stomach. Her mind was cloudy and she was moving clumsily, and she wandered off toward the river and lay down in an eddy of slow-moving water to cool the burning inside her.

For a long time she fought off drowsiness, forcing her body to rest but keeping her mind awake. The sun was going down, and the heat had gone, and the night sounds were beginning to be heard.

The birds were resting under furled feathers in their treetops, and the shadows lengthened, and the predators began to move out of their daytime lairs, searching out new tracks through the changed undergrowth, scenting the new smells.

She heard the sound of the night monkeys emerging from their shadows, a sound that told her the night had come; the effort to open her eyes was too much for her.

And soon Bichu was asleep.

chapter eight

His patience was inexhaustible.

For the Indian tomorrow was a day like any other day; the next would be the same, and the next and the next after that, because the forest and the jungle and the great wide spaces had been there for a million years and he could not know that those million years would not last forever.

And so, when he had cut the logs for the raft, Urubelava lay down to sleep while they dried out in the hot sun; it would take two days.

It was only when man left the sun—or when the cold weather, aeons ago, moved down from the poles to drive him south—that he became a slave to the science of survival. Here survival was simple. Of the world's twenty-five thousand classified plants, more than twenty thousand species grew wild in this watershed, without his care. The sun gave warmth, and there was water wherever he stepped. There were tall trees for shade, and soft-barked shrubs if he needed clothes. There was *genipa* wood for his arrows and spears, and strong fishbone for their heads. There was yellow *capi-*

rona for his cooking fires, and balsa for his rafts. There was myrrh to satisfy his craving for perfume, and towering ceibas to guide him, like landmarks, from place to place in his wanderings. There were palm fronds for his fish traps, and paralyzing poisons he could pour onto the river waters if he was too lazy to make traps. There were fruits to flavor his drinking water, and medicines without number to cure his illnesses.

And above all, perhaps, man had almost no predators. The crocodile would not harm him if he kept away from them; the deadly piranha fish were a menace only if he were foolish enough to stick a foot or an arm in among their shoals; and the one animal of any danger, the jaguar, was fed on food more easily come by, and seldom hunted man. So seldom did the jaguar hunt a man down that when he did he was called *tigre*, a name that meant a foreign animal that had no place in this gentle, nurturing bush. True, there were the insects (more insects, it would seem, than there were all over the rest of the world). But even they seemed to feed only on the intruders, the foreigners with strange tastes in their blood; they would leave the native Indian more or less alone, except, of course, on the open sandbars along the rivers, but no man in his right mind would set foot on a sandbar when he could clearly see that it was covered with a swarming black mass of millions upon millions of *pium*, the daytime mosquito, or the spike-nosed *motuca* fly, or the dreadful little *barbeiro*. The insects too would hunt him only if he were stupid enough to invade their swarming places, and to an Indian who had spent his whole life in the forests, nothing was easier than avoiding the watershed's only true danger.

Urubelava lay down and slept in a jungle clearing that would be his home till the logs had dried. When he was hungry he would hunt; and if the night grew cold he could cover himself with the blanket he himself had made; and for companionship he had his daughter, whom he loved more than anything else in the world.

He watched her now as she slowly sliced up a breadfruit she had found, moving with a kind of deliberate ease, as though she too knew that today was just a day like any other and that there was no need to hurry. She was slicing it into the cooking pot, and when she had finished she poured some river water into it and set it on the fire, and crouched over it, staring into the flames and looking up once or twice at her father with a smile while she waited for the thick white paste to reach just the right consistency. She let it cool off and then smeared it over the lower branches of a tree, where, close by, she had seen the marks of quail running in the sand. And then she too went over where her father was and lay down in the shade to doze away the rest of the day.

She thought about the *pobru bichu*, and she was saddened; but then she cheered herself with the thought of the bright-red cloth and said to her father, "When you have found the animal, we will go and look for the para trees?"

He nodded. "Of course. That is what we came here to do." He did not say any more, and she knew that if it took him a month, he would find the jaguar. It was a matter of his pride now; that, even more than the money he would get for the skin.

Before the sun went down he got up and selected the vines he would cut on the next day for binding the raft, turned the balsa logs over so that they would dry out evenly, and found a flat stone and sharpened his long knife; just before it was dark they took the three quail that had become caught in the bird lime and cooked and ate them; and then, another day like any other had gone and it was dark, so they lay down under their blankets and went to sleep.

Tomorrow, he was sure, he would find the tracks of the

animal, follow them, and kill the animal and skin it, and he would have a fine skin to take back to the village to show all his friends what a great hunter he was.

Lying awake in the night, completely covered in his blanket and living in a world of his own in the darkness underneath it, he began to worry. He could not understand how the animal had escaped from him. A jaguar so badly hurt that it could use only three of its legs and could not run far without stumbling and collapsing into a coma (he had read the tracks well), and was half-starved because all it could catch to eat was an occasional fish . . . How could such an animal evade him?

On the face of it, the answer would seem obvious: the jungle was so vast and so thick that the paths of hunter and hunted might never come together. But Urubelava was no fool. He reasoned that he could move as fast as the jaguar, that he could read and understand the marks it made as it limped and stumbled through the forest. It was merely a matter of finding the tracks once more and then, this time, not losing them. He would study each pad mark carefully, gauging the weight, and the direction, and the strength, and learning from them all there was to know about an animal that, it seemed, had deliberately set out to challenge his expertise.

But this was what he had done before, and still he had been defeated; he turned that thought over in his mind. He remembered the storm and brightened and told himself: *But for the rain, I would never have lost the tracks; and when I find them again, I will not lose them because I, Urubelava, am a man who has earned the respect of the tribe as a good hunter; I will find the tracks, and kill the animal, and take back the skin to prove to everyone that they are right in respecting me. . . .*

He shivered with the cold of the night and twisted his lithe brown body deeper into the moss. He hugged his barrel chest and curled up, his knees up under his chin, and told himself that the animal was close by, and he would find it.

Bichu, indeed, was not very far away. She had awakened and crawled to a safer place. It was as though all her instincts for caution had been blunted by pain and weariness. When this thought came to her, she would scurry as fast as she could to a recess in the rocks, or to a hole under a log, or to a crevice among the boulders; and she would spend a long time searching around her with alert eyes, scenting out the wind, making sure that this time she could safely take the sleep she so desperately needed.

And when the day came, she awoke with the humid scent of warm wood around her, and the tangy smell of the ferns, and she yelped in pain as she stretched her lovely long limbs; and then she was alert as all the memories came back to her.

She could smell food close by. Her stomach was empty, but when she began to crawl toward the smell, her hindquarters were dragging painfully, not responding promptly to the commands of her brain. There was unaccustomed sound as she moved through the night-damp grasses, and she heard the scuffling as an animal—and she did not even see what it was—scurried away from her approach. She moved on and investigated the scent, finding the tracks of a tapir, four-toed in front and three in the rear; there was a pile of half-eaten palm nuts on the ground, and when she raised her head she could hear the ugly, snub-trunked animal snorting as it plunged into the water nearby. She turned to follow it, limping painfully and forcing herself to control those recalcitrant rear legs, for the tapir moved slowly and she was sure that, even now, she could catch it easily. She stumbled along the track it had forced through the bushes, and when she came to the water's edge it was standing there in the shallows, a little way from the bank, turning back to look at her.

The scent of it was strong, and she plunged into the water after it, the hunger gnawing at her. The water here was covered thickly with a wet mat of green leaves and yellow water lilies, so that only her head was visible among them as they swirled to let her body pass and then closed ranks again behind her; her head was a brown-and-white ball in the mass of floating flowers. But the tapir dived and was gone long before she reached midstream. It would be a long time under water and would surface a long way away. She dragged herself back out of the weeds and onto dry land, and she lay down again to rest, even though she had slept so recently. Her alertness was gone, and even her will to live was slowly seeping out of her, renewing itself from time to time and then fading and leaving her slack and comatose. And each time, it seemed, the lassitude was more deadly than it had been before.

There was no way of knowing when these spiritless periods would come over her. Her intellect was an animal intellect, and she could know only what her heredity had taught her—that death comes to those who meekly accept it. And so she drove herself ever harder.

It was her instinct, nonetheless, that made her now seek out a strongly scented herb that Urubelava would have called *pijicapu* and sometimes used as a narcotic. As a sick cat chews grass, Bichu chewed on the atropinic plant to ease the intestinal spasms that were causing her so much suffering. Her mouth was dry with the astringency of it, but she was slowly anesthetized from pain and soon felt strong enough to lie down on the bank with one paw in the water, waiting for an unwary fish.

Her first stroke was not quick enough, nor her second or third or fourth; but at last she swept a large black corbina out of the water and fastened her teeth on it; and when she had eaten, though hardly enough, she slunk off along the grassy overhung bank, moving faster now, searching out the landmarks that would guide her to her home on the other side of the river.

Soon the river swung around in a broad arc, and the roar in her ears was the sound of a waterfall; she knew this sound and this place. She looked around instinctively for an immense red anthill that had always been here, and found it, toppled over by the recent floods and broken up but still crawling with millions of tiny white ants. She steered around them; they would cover her in moments, biting into her fur with their sharp, microscopic teeth, searching out the smooth skin underneath. She looked for a thick cluster of myrrh trees she knew was there, sniffing out the ripe, rich scent of them and then moving over to where her nose told her they would be, although they could not be seen; she found them toppled over by the rains and saw that a yellow-beaked toucan was clawing at one of the upturned roots. The toucan peered at her myopically from its high perch, jerking its neck from side to side, and then flew off, calling out a raucous, honking alarm.

Bichu moved on, searching.

A little farther on she came to the edge of the waterfall, where the rolling river, white-flecked, poured over the edge of the broken rocks to plunge straight down for a hundred feet or more, to boil and froth in the green pool below. A great flat slab of granite at the edge of the falls, halfway across, sent its own individual spout of water shooting out like the stream pouring from a kettle. And a little way down the sheer drop, a jagged outcrop of yellow rock was formed like a balanced cup that held just enough soggy earth to house a dozen long, trailing lilies of brilliant crimson that cascaded down to the edge of the falling water.

On the edge of the cup a fat *hoatzin* pheasant, dark red and white, was perched, pondering the effort it would take to fly back to dry land, eyeing the falling water; the hooked claws that unpredictable nature had placed at the top of its wings were curled over the lip of the rock, holding on firmly. It turned its bright-crested head to watch the approaching jaguar, fluttering its long eyelashes, and then turned and dived under the water and was gone. Bichu watched it dive, knowing that not long ago she could have sprung out there and taken her meal before the clumsy, foolish bird could have even heard her approach.

The *hoatzin* was a remarkable bird, a bird that hated the effort of flying and was more at home underwater than it was in the sky. It would swim under the water like a fish, and then, clambering out onto the shore with its bright feathers wet and bedraggled, it would use its wing claws to climb like a lizard up to its crude stick nest in the lower branches that overhung the river.

The roar of the falls was loud and insistent here, and to Bichu it was a source of great comfort. The waterfall, and the scented myrrh, and even the toppled red anthill, were all familiar steps to her home, where the granite cave and the banana trees were. Her body stretched out on the cool grasses, with her head held back and her long tail delicately flicking, she saw hundreds of scarlet ibises circle against the

sky, brilliant red splashing the bright, bright blue where puffs of white clouds drifted.

The boulders that lined the edge of the falls were shining in the sunlight; they were a sure and easy path across to the other side. There were a few flat stones where the water had gouged its way between them, and then that large, sharply sloping slab of gray granite that stuck its long nose out of the water, and then a deep, wide gap that had to be jumped, and then a huge tree that was wedged among the rocks at the edge, and then a narrow gorge where the water thundered, and then the opposite bank with the pampas beyond it and the mountain beyond that.

She had crossed here many times; it was all familiar. The feeling for her home was strong in her, and she began to cross.

She stood with her forefeet on the edge of the rocks, the water moving fast and boiling under her belly. She brought her rear paws over to the rocks and stood there, delicately balanced. Her four paws were very close together as she gathered herself for the leap to the sloping granite, the water glistening on it brightly. Somewhere close by a parrot began to call, chattering loudly; and a monkey screeched, calling to its young. But the sounds of the forest were drowned out by the roar of the water as it thundered down to the pool; the air was damp with wind-borne spray.

She tried her bad leg, putting a little weight on it. Strangely, the pain was in her neck now, and she eased her head from side to side, and when she coughed she felt the almost-forgotten pain in her ribs.

For a long time she stood there, remembering the leap she had failed to make farther down the river where the crocodiles were and how frightening it had been not to be able to manage such a simple thing. She gauged the distance

to the sloping rock, and then she stepped back on the bank
again and lay down and waited, without knowing what she
was waiting for.

Her home was over there, far away but across the river,
and soon she got to her feet again and once more took up
that delicately poised position on the flat rocks. She leaped
out onto the granite and felt the cold wet surface of it under
her pads. She slipped a little and there was a moment of
panic; but now she was safely in midstream, with the worst
behind her. She spread her legs wide and held herself firmly,
looking back at the churning water behind her, looking
down over the steep edge to the pool far below.

The edge of the falls turned here, making a sharp angle
and jutting out to her right, so that now she was crossing
farther away from the lip itself; and here the water was
smooth and rolling, moving fast but unflecked with the
white foam; and she could see a large fat fish, caught in the
too strong current, sweeping under a foot of water toward
the edge. A heavy log was caught here, half under the water,
and she reached out and tried it, withdrawing the probing
paw when its tremor became more marked. A tangle of
branches came sweeping downstream and over the edge, and
then she stared long and hard at the big tree beyond the
wide gap, knowing that this she could safely clamber over.

But first, the gap. . . .

Her body slipped back gently onto the haunches as she
gathered herself for the spring. Her front paws were outstretched, her rear legs tucked under her, as she tensed her
muscles. And then, like a spring unleashing itself, her long
body shot out and she was in midair, her forelegs reaching,
her rear legs held well back for maximum balance; even her
tail was held just so as her front paws reached out for, and
found, the scattered, broken rocks that were to be her foot-

hold. One leg was deep in the water, up to her shoulder, and she could feel the overwhelming force of the water; but her other legs were firm, and in a moment she was on the roots of the sodden tree, clawing at it and pulling herself clear, moving up its ancient trunk—who could tell how long it had been there, slowly dying?—until she was well clear of the rushing water.

She paused to flex her strained muscles, to gasp air into her pounding lungs and ease the deep pain in her belly. She felt herself leaning into one of the wet branches to stifle the pain.

She was safe now. The wide valley here swept back on both sides from the river, a deep green glade with broad borders of lush foliage, with the trees standing high a little way back from the river, and then the rising slope of the land that led to the mountains on both sides. It was as though the earth had sliced itself open here to let the river through, and all the greenery that grew along its banks.

She held onto her high perch with sharp claws and looked around her, over the green valley and the water, listening to the friendly roar of the falls.

And then the angle of the branches she was on began to change. One side was gently, almost reluctantly, moving down into the water; the other side, where her back legs were, was rising fast, and she spun around and found a new footing. And then, as she began to leap to the land that was now so near, the trunk toppled and crashed and upended itself, rearing high out of the water, towering momentarily on the edge of the fall like a god rising out of the water. For a second or two it hung there; its roots, now reaching down again, seemed to probe into the fast water to find something to grasp onto.

And then the water took it.

There was a grinding, tearing sound as a thick root, long wedged under the rocks, sheared off; and the giant tree crashed down over the steep drop of the falls. And, somewhere among its roots, fighting for life, Bichu found herself deep underwater, her lungs only half full, her body tearing itself apart with unbearable pain; the pressure of the water was exploding her head, and she was trying to shriek and hold her breath at the same time, twisting herself around and around and trying to fight her way clear of the tangled roots that now seemed like living tentacles strangling her and forcing her under the water.

She was up out of the river as the tree spun over again, high above the surface and falling; she could see the drop of the water far to one side of her, and when she struggled to right herself the pool was down below, racing up to meet her.

It seemed an eternity that she hung there, her limbs reaching out and pawing the air as she fell; she was conscious of the sound of a scream and knew that it came from her own throat. And then she struck.

The water drove out the air with rushing sound, and she was sinking in the green water, twisting herself and feeling the pounding of flesh inside her. Her eyes were open, but she could see nothing. She felt herself hit the bottom of the pool, the jagged rocks striking hard at the back of her neck and sending her body spinning; and then the water sent her shooting up to the surface again, and she opened her mouth and gulped in a great breath of air, and, incredibly, she was still alive. Her body was numb; her legs were flailing, not doing what she wanted them to do. She was on her back again, turning again, and water was flooding her lungs; she tried to strike out for the trees she could see, but the whirlpool had her in its grasp, sending her spinning around like a toy. She tried to roll herself up into a ball, letting her instinct have its way, burying her muzzle in her own stomach; and then the water thrust her out of its grip, sending her sprawling toward the edge of the pool, twisting like a piece of garbage caught up in the maelstrom; it spewed her toward the wet land, and now soft mud was under her back, and all motion was stilled.

For a long time she did not move; she was not able even to force herself farther away from the edge of the water. And when at last she uncurled herself, she was on the muddied bank and the trees and shrubs flashed like bright lights, the yellows and reds and purples that were the orchids in the trees and the explosions in her head mixed together in one terrifying nightmare.

She felt the mud all around her; she was deeply embedded in it. And then the pains exploded beyond endurance and she could not stifle the whimpering; she lost consciousness altogether, and the whole world was dark and silent.

High in the trees above her a troupe of monkeys was gathering nervously to stare down at her. One of them, just a few weeks old, was whining softly. Bichu lay curled up in the mud, a brown-and-yellow ball of wet fur with the water rushing and pounding past her, and to her even the roar of the falls was silent now.

chapter nine

He had told himself that he would find the tracks, and he did.

Or rather, one of the strange gods he sometimes worshiped came to his rescue, he was sure, as he stood knee-deep in the black mud maneuvering the cumbersome, lightweight raft over a barrier of rocks where the white water was running too fast for safety. The falls, he knew, were ahead of him, and though he was not frightened of them, he knew that he needed all his skill to keep the fragile balsa logs from shooting out from under him. He was accustomed to the use of the light raft in the water; it was a quick and easy way of moving around in this great basin where the rivers were so numerous that a man could never hope to count them. Water and tangled green vegetation—he was at home in either of them, however far from his true home he might be.

With the crude paddle he had made with his *facao* he had steered the raft carefully over to the edge of the river, where the mud and the weeds would slow him. There the raft would stick from time to time in the mud or on the shallow rocks and allow his strong hands to hold it steady while the water was trying to tear it away from him. It was all a matter of custom, and done with ease.

He had cut a long rope of vines and slung it to his daughter to tie to one of the branches that hung low over the water, so that the raft would swing on it gently, a few yards at a time, easing its way toward the narrow tributary that lay to one side just before the main branch of the river cascaded down into the great hole, where, he knew, the devils of the forest lived.

The young girl, almost up to her waist in mud and water, pulling the heavy vine over her thin shoulder (it was almost as thick as her forearm), stopped to stare at the ground close by.

A brightly colored bird had died, and a dried-out wing, still brilliant with red and gaudy blue, was sprayed out like a fan in a tangle of yellow-green liana that hung down, almost touching the water, from a tall stand of hymenaea gum; the gum trees caught his eye because this was the wood he burned to pacify the evil spirits with its sweet aroma, and he thought at first she was examining it to see if perhaps they should cut some to help find the jaguar. But it was not the gum she was staring at, nor even the bright feathers which normally would have pleased and excited her; it was something so important that even the feathers meant nothing to her.

In a moment she glanced back toward him and then looked away hurriedly, almost guiltily, and went on tugging at the heavy rope and moving it toward the strong anchor point of a dalbergia root.

He called out, "What is it, daughter? The gum? I see it." She did not answer him, and there was something strange about the way she would not look at him, as though she were making up her mind to lie, which was something she did not often do.

He waited till she had secured the rope, and he let the raft swing free, and then, instead of following it in its curving path as it swept on to the end of the rope, swinging wildly, he went over to the red-and-blue feathers. The fast flow of water made broad waves around his heavy chest, and when he reached the bank he saw them.

There was a series of deep, clearly etched pad marks in the mud, six, seven, eight—more of them than he could count—leading onto the rocks by the edge of the river. He saw at once that the two rear pads were strong, that one of the front paws was barely touching the ground, that the pad marks were improperly spaced as though the animal were limping, and he said softly, "It is my jaguar." There were a thousand, a hundred thousand, jaguars in the forest; but this one, to his skilled eye, was as distinctive from all the others as one man is from his neighbor.

He looked over at his daughter. She had sunk to the ground and was sitting there, dejected, her long child's legs tucked under her, her brown fingers in her lap, gently stroking each other; she would not look at him, and it made him very sad, sadder almost than the lie of her silence.

For a moment he thought he ought to strike her, just once and not really very hard. But he decided not to, and instead he said quite gently, although he was angry, "Does an animal mean more to you than your own father?"

She began to cry, and he could not tell how many of the tears were for the lie and how many for the *pobru bichu.* He said, "Come. We will follow the tracks now."

She got to her feet slowly, and looked at the raft, and asked, "Shall I move the rope again?"

He nodded his head vigorously, which meant no, and said, "We do not need the raft anymore."

"We must not leave it there."

"I know that." If some passing *desatitos* should find it . . . He splashed over to the rope and sliced it through with one blow of his knife, and the raft that had taken him nearly two days to build was caught in the current and went sweeping on over the rocks toward the falls. He laughed as it stood momentarily on its end, balanced there on a rock by the whims of the river, and then rose up in the air and hung there for a minute before it crashed down again and began to break up. He said, pointing at the sight, "Let the devils have it!"

Now she too was laughing. Her sadness was gone as quickly as it had come, and she knew what he was laughing about; for just a brief instant the upended raft, already breaking apart, had looked like Akuriba's house the time it fell down just after he had built it. Akuriba was a neighbor in the village who never seemed to be able to do anything right, and his fallen house had been a subject of amusement for a long time, and now, with the long poles just beginning to separate from their bindings, the raft had looked exactly like it. He said, shouting with laughter, "The house of Akuriba, you remember?"

It was one of the little amusements that would never be forgotten.

He stared for a long time at the tracks in the mud, noticing that there was no blood anymore and that the paws on the side of his spear arm were uncertain. There was one place where all four pad marks were evenly distributed, and he said, "Ah, she is trying to use all her legs again, but she still cannot run properly."

When the tracks petered out among the rocks, he carefully marked the last one with a tall stick that he could easily see from a distance, and then he made a wide circle around it, studying the ground intently, then widening the circle when, the first time, he found nothing. On the third cast he found some grass that had been bent down by a heavy weight, and a broken twig, and a little farther on he found a scarred tree trunk where claws had recently scratched.

He put some more sticks in the ground by the pad marks and looked at the line they made, and then moved along the main course of the river, not looking back at his daughter but knowing that she was close behind, following silently and a little ashamed of her recent behavior. He lost the tracks again very soon and sat down for a long while to think; and when he began to cast again he soon found a broken anthill, covered over with white termites, where a million ants were feasting on some drying-out fishbones.

Crouching to study the ground, putting his face close to the grass and peering at it along the angle, he said, "She lay down here by the pool and fished for a while. She caught a *corbina* and ate it. And then she moved on, this way, toward the white water where the rocks are." He found the tracks of a tapir, with a new set of pad marks close behind. He said, quite sure of himself, "No! This is not the way she was moving. She turned here to hunt a tapir, but she could not catch even a beast that moves so slowly." He said, "She will die soon if she does not eat. An animal cannot live without food, like a man; it will die, and then the vultures will take it and there will be no skin to sell for money." He looked back the way he had come and said, pointing, "Over there; she went that way, toward the falls."

He was moving faster now, almost running, looking up at the scarlet ibises that were circling high in the blue sky, circling as though they would never move from this place, gliding slowly, silently along on broad, outstretched wings that reflected the sunlight.

He came to the granite edge of the falls, and he crouched on his heels and read all the signs carefully and then stood up and stared at the bank on the other side. He said, "This is where she crossed the river."

She answered him, puzzled, "Why should an animal want to cross the river? One side is the same as the other."

He looked at her and laughed and said, "You are a foolish woman. The animal is going to its home, to the mountains on the other side. It does not know that it will die before it can reach them. It does not know that Urubelava will come with his arrows and kill it. With one arrow, I tell you." He touched a thick, stubby finger to the side of his neck and said, "Here, in the neck, this is where I will shoot it. And the skin will not be spoiled."

They stood together now, looking down at the spray-misted pool far below, half hidden by green and yellow foliage through which the water poured in fearsome strength; a rainbow reached up out of the water here and buried its other end among the trees on the far bank; the roar of the water was almost insupportable, and they had to shout to make themselves heard above it. The girl saw that her father was eyeing the rocks that led across the edge, gauging the distances between them, calculating the steps they would have to take; she could not repress a shudder, and she hoped he would not see that she was afraid.

He said, "Wait here." He pulled out his knife and walked into the forest, and when he came back he was cleaning the twigs off a long pole of cesalpina wood, like an oversized spear, peeling off the bark and smoothing it at one end. He said again, "Wait here."

She sat down to watch as he stepped onto the flat stones

and prodded the rocks ahead of him with the pole, testing their stability. He jumped quickly over the gap, onto a sloping slab of gray granite that was wetly shining and slippery; but his great splayed feet held firmly, the toes almost prehensile. He stood there, poised on the brink like a mountain goat, surefooted and confident, unafraid of the pounding water below him. He used his pole again to feel the water ahead of him, pushing it down deep and not finding bottom, then pulling it out again and standing there leaning on it nonchalantly while he scratched the scars on his belly and wondered about his daughter.

He crossed back to the bank at last and cut a length of vine and gave it to her to twist around her narrow waist, and then, laughing at her fear, he crossed with her onto the big granite slab, helping her half-jump, half-step across the deep water onto it. And then they stood there looking ahead of them, and at last he took one end of her rope and jumped easily across onto a cluster of white stones that were so sharp they cut into the thick leather of his bare feet, and he turned back and called out to her over the roar of the falls, "Now! Jump!"

Obediently she jumped as far and as high as she could. She felt the sharp tug of the rope around her waist, and then the stones were cutting her feet too and she stumbled and fell; but the rope was taut around her body and her father was hauling on it hard, pulling her to her feet. She cut her hands on the stones and laughed because he was laughing and was suddenly sobered when she looked down into the distant pool, so very far below them. He said, "The rest is easy now, two quick steps, one two . . ." He still had the long pole, and he prodded the water to show her that here the river was fast but very shallow. But he still held the end of the rope as she ran quickly over the rocks, feeling the rush of the water around her ankles, and then he followed her, and they both dropped down to the wet grass on the other side.

For a long time, thinking of the way they might have both slipped and fallen down among the devils in the wet pit below them, he did not stop laughing. In Urubelava's world there was nothing funnier than a calamity that didn't quite happen.

He got up soon and began to cast around for the animal's tracks, and when he did not find them at once he looked up at the sun and said, "There is time. First we will eat; then we will find the animal."

He drew his knife and sharpened the pole at one end, putting a very fine point on it, and he went over to a little tributary where the water was running slower but still fast enough to be clear, and he stood there with his sharp pole upraised; at his first throw he brought out a fine *arapaima*, more than four feet long and weighing so much that he had to call to her to help him land it. He built a fire and lit it while she cleaned the big, oily fish with his knife, and when it was cooked, still on the pole that had run it through, they sat and ate until they could eat no more; there was still a lot of it left for the vultures and the ants and the jackals.

And then, when he suddenly noticed the blood on his daughter's feet, he remembered how they had both cut themselves on the sharp stones, and he began to rub wood ash methodically into their wounds.

There was plenty of time to catch up with the animal, now that they knew where it must have left, on this side of the river, some signs for him to read. When he had rested awhile and savored in retrospect the excitement of crossing the falls, he would begin his search for the tracks again. Given a starting point, there was no animal alive that would not leave a track clear enough for him to find if he set his mind on it.

And this was where the *bichu* had crossed; the pad marks across the river told the story. And where else could it go, if not to here?

But first a little repose, a little time to enjoy the pleasures of the day. The rest would come later.

The first thought that came to Bichu as she came back to her senses was that her rear legs were gone; she could not feel them at all.

The movement of her forepart, the turning of her shoulders, caused no movement beyond the smooth upcurve of her belly at the narrowest part of her long body. She panicked when her rear legs would not obey the commands of her brain, but were dragged out of the sticky mud only by her powerful shoulders, which tugged them along uselessly. The legs were twisted under her, dragging on their sides, her once-powerful paws useless.

These were the killing legs that doubled up under her belly like steel springs, that could slash out with enormous power, with sharp claws for defense or to find food. They could be drawn up and back and sent striking out with the speed of lightning, and there was a great rhythmic beauty in their ease of movement. And now they trailed behind her, scuffling along the ground as she pulled her shoulders forward, crawling very slowly, for cover; she was whining, not with the pain, for the pain was already a part of her life now, but with the sense of helplessness that left her closer to death than she had ever been before.

Instinctively she looked up above her, remembering the vultures and the big condor she had killed with a rapid slash of those legs. But there was nothing except the dense mist of the spray and the heavy, shining green foliage. And over everything was the pounding, incessant roar of the falls that had carried her down to this dank and dismal place.

She could not know how long she had been there unconscious; she knew only that the hunger pains had come back again and that there was nothing she could do now to assuage them. The hunger was a growing thing; a bird, a few small fish—these were not enough, over the accumulation of the last few days, to keep up the strength that she needed now if she were to survive. And survival was the instinct that was drumming into her consciousness, driving away the pain and frustration.

Man had escaped nature's cruelty by his civilization; when the realization of that cruelty had fully come upon him, his efforts had subjugated nature, and sometimes he could turn its terrors to his own account; but for the animals there was only a long and losing struggle against a forest and a jungle in which, in the best times, they were assured of safety and contentment, but where, once their powers were impaired in the slightest, they would quickly become part of the forest's constant search for food to rot down into humus; they too soon, when they were weakened, became victims of the relentless ecology of their surroundings.

She pulled herself heavily in among the thick, well-watered bushes, seeking first to hide herself because her weakness was acute and she was helpless against any of the dangers that might threaten her. She lay on her side and tried to move her useless legs, tried to twist them around from under her; but she could not. She used her front legs, even the one that hurt her so much, to pull herself deeper into the cover

of cool ferns that hid her from the rest of the world and en-
abled her to find the solitude that she needed; and she
fought with all her willpower against the lassitude that was
still on her. She looked around her at the dark greenery;
she did not know this place. The air was heavy with spray,
and it was quite cold; her fur was soaked with a dampness
that seemed to search its way right through her bones. There
was no sign of level land anywhere; on every side of her
there were steep, slippery banks, where tiny rivulets ran
down, cutting deep gorges in the sand.

She could see a snake, thick-bodied, flat-headed, long and
striped in yellow and gray. It was a fer-de-lance, and it was
one of the few snakes that would attack her for no reason;
it was watching her, turning its head slowly as she moved
away, its strange eyes fixed on her own; the eyes had pupils
like a cat's; she looked away and dragged herself deeper into
the bushes, feeling now the scraping of her paws as she
dragged them over a patch of thorn. She reached out with
both front legs and curled her claws around a thick palm
stub and pulled herself bodily up toward it; and when she
looked back, the snake had gone; she had not heard its
slithering. The palms were dark with a cluster of burgundy-
colored vipers, ten, twelve, more of them, coiled around the
bulbous nodes. She did not like snakes, although most would
not harm her unless they were disturbed. But she knew that
in her present condition she could easily blunder into them
and start them coiling, ready to strike. She saw *coralitos,* and
anacondas, and a fer-de-lance, all of which, she knew, would
attack her with the slightest provocation. It was an un-
healthy place for her, and she feared it. She looked up out
of the dark pit and knew that somehow she must make the
climb up its slippery, treacherous slopes.

She dragged herself upward, moving with pathetic slow-

ness up the wet bank, sinking her front claws into the wet
earth and contracting her shoulder muscles till the head
moved forward a few inches, then reaching out to pull again.
It was terribly slow, painful, and laborious.

Soon she was close to the top, and the sun struck obliquely
across her; she had not seen it for a very long time. A stinging cloud of insects, of a kind she had never seen before, was
hanging around her eyes, troubling her because she could
not shake herself free of them; and now, with the sun, they
left her to go her own way and went back to the dark wet
depths where they lived; some of them had entered her eyes,
which were watering badly. She scraped her head along the
wet grass at the top, trying to rub the irritation away.

At last she could see the mountains in the far distance—
dark blue and purple, with golden streaks where the sun was
striking against them. It seemed farther away than it had
ever been before, but she knew that she was still another
step nearer to her home. There was the jungle, a day's run
when she was fit; and then there were the wide pampas; and
then the mountains began, and high up in those mountains
was her home.

She lay on her side again and rested, and she tried once
more to move her rear legs; they were still in paralysis. She
heard a rustling sound and smelled food; a pair of unsus-
pecting *cariacu* deer strolled past her, nibbling at the tender
shoots of an acacia. She was sure they had seen her; the male
had stopped his browsing and was staring straight at her,
but there was no fear in his eyes. Was her helplessness, then,
so complete that even a timid *cariacu* could see it? She tried
to twist herself around, and suddenly the two deer bounded
away, seeking safety in the thickets; she heard them racing
off, crashing away through the foliage until they were gone.
She licked at her lips; she needed food.

The sun had already begun to sink, and soon the darkness came, with all the noises of the night; she lay shivering under a heavy log, listening to the sounds of the nighttime animals all around her. She heard the hunting roar of another jaguar, a long way off; close by she heard a yapock, the water opossum, splashing about in the shallows of the river. She dragged herself painfully toward the sound, but when she reached the edge of the water the sounds had gone and she knew that she had been heard. A tawny marmosa, rodent-tailed and black-masked like a nighttime bandit, was prowling in the tree above her, hunting out sleeping butterflies for food. A tribe of *douroucouli* monkeys, red-furred and tufted-tailed, were hunting insects, picking them delicately out of the tree bark all around her. She slept, hungry and craving food almost as much as she craved the safety of the shelter she had found.

And then, in the early morning, an amazing thing happened.

As she lay there, she could smell the scent of her own kind. The glaze went from her eyes as she forced herself into full awareness, and she twisted so that the joints of her front legs were directly under her long body, raising up her head to peer out from under the log. She could see nothing. Slowly she dragged herself forward; and at the noise she made, the slight sounds she had heard stopped abruptly. Knowing the danger signals, she too stopped all movement, even the movement of her head. Her eyes darted from side to side, searching. And then she saw them.

Two small jaguars, not more than a few weeks old, were standing there watching her, their plump little bodies standing straight on firm legs, looking back over their shoulders at her with alert, inquiring eyes. For a long time they did not move. And then one of them—it was a male—came over cautiously and sniffed at her, darting its head forward quickly and then retreating as though alarmed, but coming back again to sniff and inquire, it seemed, why she did not answer his movements.

The other came over and joined its mate; it was a female. They sniffed at her cautiously, and one of them put out a paw and tapped her on the nose lightly; and when she did not play with them they began to whine. They raced off together and then raced back again, colliding with her clumsily and rolling over her. The play went on for a long long time, and then they moved away and looked at her; and all the time she had not moved. They could not understand why she did not respond to their teasing, and they stood there looking away into the forest as though they were not interested, and then looking at her quickly to see if perhaps she would glance at them or make a movement as soon as their attentions were elsewhere. One of them yawned broadly, and then they wandered off among the waving green ferns.

When they had gone, Bichu fell asleep again. And soon, she felt their presence once more as they nestled up against her, and it was dark, and the night had come again. The hunger was gnawing deeply into her now, and it was all the worse because she could smell the ripe scent of fresh food nearby. She lay on her side with her head on the grass, breathing heavily as the two young ones romped about her, stumbling over her body, putting out tentative claws to pat at her muzzle, and sometimes whining when she seemed to ignore them.

They went off again to find some sport in the jungle, and Bichu felt the dreaded coma coming over her, and she fought against it.

And then, suddenly, there was food.

She scented it first, and then she heard the rustling of the bushes. In the darkness, the baby male was dragging a haunch of a young tapir, freshly killed; it was quite a small one, not much older than the two cubs; the young had killed the young; it was part of the process of the forest's life, that those who could not survive should shed their blood to sustain those who could. The cub dragged the meat closer to Bichu, straining his short, stubby rear legs, and he dropped it close by her head. Behind him, the young female licked her lips and yawned again to show her lack of interest, and Bichu rolled over and stretched out a paw and dragged the meat in close and crunched her teeth on it hungrily.

The two young animals stayed with her, watching her eat. When the sun had risen high and the jungle was steaming with heat, they went away quietly and did not come back. Refreshed, her stomach filled with good sustaining meat for the first time in countless days and nights, Bichu slept again.

In her sleep, she stretched her rear legs, not even waking to learn that the strength was coming back into the bruised muscles and pinched nerves. And when yet another night had come, she moved slowly out of her lair and stood looking at the moonlit forest, watching the shadows and the bright patches of blue light; and then, quite firmly, limping only a little, she moved off into the jungle.

She was heading for the pampas and the mountain.

chapter ten

His puzzlement showed clearly as he screwed up his tiny black eyes, squinting as though the hot sun were too much for them; he scratched his chin, and turned his head this way and that, and stared at the stones and the mud and the sand and the grasses; and he crouched down and touched the soil lightly as though his fingers could tell him more than his sharp eyes could, and then stood up again and clicked his tongue noisily, and wagged his head from side to side, unbelieving.

He had done this a dozen times, standing there in the bright sunlight and shaking his head, and then casting around where he had already cast before and found nothing. His daughter knew that this was something her father understood well and now was not able to cope with; the way he fingered his thick lips worried her, because she knew that it meant he was worried too.

He said at last, not really trying to teach her but wanting to explain the problem to someone, "Look at this patch of mud; look at it." His finger pointing down to it, he walked back to the edge of the falls, then followed the mud patch around where it flared away from the water in a soil depression, all the way to where it swung back and met the river again. It made a semicircle a hundred yards or so across, with each end anchored on the water that fed it and kept it damp; it was soft, black, gelatinous mud that might have become another tiny tributary had it been powerful enough to move away the sludge.

He raised his finger and said, "Now look again, carefully," and he went all the way back again, checking to see that she was following, was watching his didactic gesture as he traced the line of the mud. He said, "You understand what this means? The animal could not leave the water without crossing the mud. All the land on this side of the river is enclosed by the marsh here; you see it? From the water there"—pointing—"to the water there"—pointing again—"all this piece of land we stand on is surrounded by a strip of mud, like the ditch that Akuriba tried to build around his house, remember?" This time he did not laugh about Akuriba; there was too much puzzling him, and in his world anything he did not understand was a source of considerable worry. He said, "Where an animal crosses mud, it leaves its tracks for a wise man to follow. Am I not right?"

She nodded vigorously; the assumption that her father was wrong was impossible. He said, throwing his arms wide and making a dramatic gesture of it, "And yet, there are no tracks. We saw where the animal crossed the river. Am I not right? It cannot swim against the force of the water and come out farther upstream. Even if it were strong it could not do this, because the water is too fast. And it is not strong; it is wounded. It cannot go over the edge, because that way it would be killed. And so . . . it must have landed just here, where your father stands now." Again, that dramatic gesture. "Then where is it now? It must be here, among the bushes. Perhaps it is dead. We will search."

(Before he started to talk to her, he had already searched and found nothing; but he wanted to make absolutely sure.) Together they parted the leaves of the bushes, the fronds of the ferns; they closely examined every inch of the space that was enclosed by the circle of mud, and when they had finished, he said in renewed astonishment, "You see? The animal is not here. It did not leave this place, but it is not here."

She too began to scratch at her body, puzzling it all out. She said at last, "The animal went over the edge of the falls."

For a long time he did not answer her, and then he said gravely, at last, "This is what I have already decided. The animal went over the falls."

Now there was the great problem: what to do about it, even if so unlikely a supposition were true. He began to be sorry he had claimed the idea as his own, because now he would have to follow it up. He wished he had told her scornfully, *How could an animal go over the falls; it would be killed. . . .* But then he realized that perhaps this had indeed happened, and that the jaguar was down there waiting for the vultures or the devils, or someone with a sharp knife who could come along and skin it before the other predators got there. Thinking more about it, he began to nod his head wisely, glancing at his daughter and making up his mind. She now knew what he wanted to do, and she was terrified. He saw her fear and said gently, "You will stay here. I will go down and look."

"But the devils?"

He said, "I will protect myself. You will find me some *yucuchu.*"

It was a thick, fleshy plant that grew freely here by the

edge of the river, a bright-yellow, pulpy plant that looked, and was, deadly poisonous. He watched his daughter go off along the bank in search of some, and then he went into the forest and shot a toucan with his bow, and tied a thin piece of vine around its legs, and walked back along the river to just the right kind of pool he had already noted, and there he dropped the toucan into the water, holding on to the end of the vine so as not to lose it.

Nothing happened; he pulled it out and tried again farther upriver; and then again; and on the sixth try he found what he wanted. There was a sudden flurry in the water as a shoal of piranhas attacked the dead bird with their razor-sharp teeth; in less than fifteen seconds the agitation stopped, and Urubelava hauled out at the end of his cord what was left of the bait; there was nothing but the bone-white skeleton.

Handling it very carefully so that it would not break apart too much, he went back along the river to his daughter. She had already cut some *yucuchu* and was heating it in the pot with some water, stirring it vigorously with a stick; the stock was a brilliant ocher-yellow. He nodded his approval, examined it carefully, and said, "Enough."

Very carefully, using a bunch of grass as a paintbrush, he began to stain the white bones of the toucan. Soon it was finished, and he hung it in the branches of a tree to dry. He sat down on his heels, saying nothing, and when the stain was dry and brilliant, he broke off some of the bright yellow bones, threaded a piece of thin vine through them, and hung the necklace around his neck. He said, "Wash out the pot well, or the spirits will be angry with us."

She was already scouring the yellow stain with wet sand. To tell the truth, she did not really believe in all this ritual with the bones, and as for spirits who might get angry over

an uncleansed pot . . . But a missionary had once told her
that people could die from eating out of pots in which *yucuchu* had been boiled. And although she did not believe in
the superstition, she knew that her father did; and perhaps,
after all, he was as right in this, as he was in most things; it
did not hurt to be careful.

And so she scrubbed hard with the sand and he said
gruffly, very conscious of the courage he was showing in front
of his daughter, "Wait for me here. I will climb down to
the hole where the devils are and see if the *bichu* is there."
He saw the worry on her face, and he touched his yellow
necklace and said, "The demons will not harm me. I am
protected."

He spent a little time sharpening his *facao* on a smooth
stone, testing it when it was ready on the thick nail of his
thumb, and then he began the long climb down into the pit
where the water fell.

The thunder of the water here scared him, and he looked
back over his shoulder at every step, touching the yellow
bones around his neck and muttering over and over again,
"*Yucuchu, yucuchu, yucuchu* . . ." At each step he grew
more frightened, more sorry that he had so rashly boasted
to his daughter of his courage; it was a terrifyingly long way
to the pool below, splashing up its water and casting rain-
bows everywhere, and the roar grew louder still as he de-
scended, quite deafening him. There were gray rocks,
washed clean by the spray, and shiny leaves of plants he had
never seen before; he wondered if they were the food the
devils ate.

The way down was steep and muddy and treacherous. A
great boulder that he was clinging to came away and thundered down the slope, and he grabbed for support at a
thorny vine that was covered with a million stinging red

ants; he had dropped his bow, and the first thing he did when he recovered his balance was to search for it, because in this dreadful place, without a bow, he was a dead man. He saw it lodged in the upper branches of a tall spindly tree, and he slithered down to its base and climbed up like a monkey to recover it. He saw a fer-de-lance there; its gray-green banded body was enormous, more than seven feet long, and it was weaving its head from side to side. This was its home, its territory, and he was the intruder; he knew that it was ready to strike. In panic he struck out and slashed off its head with his knife, glad now that he had the wisdom to sharpen it. And when he slid back down the tree and clambered down to the bottom over the broken water-shining rocks, he put a foot carelessly into a stand of new reeds and felt a painful sting on his ankle.

He shrieked out his alarm, sure that a devil had taken him, in spite of his necklace, and when he pulled his foot back he saw that a deadly little *coralito*, the Brazilian cobra, had taken hold of him; he could feel the rapid vibration of the biting, the back teeth grinding while the front teeth hung on; it was like a burn moving rapidly over the length of his foot. He slashed out quickly with his knife, instinctively, knowing that no snake, not even a *coralito* was a devil, and therefore he, a man, could save himself from it if he moved fast enough. The snake would not let go; it hung on to him like a long and evil leech, and the blade turned on its tough, shining red scales. So he grabbed it firmly and cut off its tail, and then slid the knife down his foot, slicing through the blunt head at the jawbone.

There would be others in that patch of grass and he dragged himself quickly away from it, falling down on a patch of wet moss and already feeling the pain in his eyes. He sliced at his flesh quickly and tried to bring his foot up to his mouth to suck out the poison; but the bites were on the wrong side of his ankle and he could not get them to his lips. He made three more cuts on this foot, very deep across the wound, and he picked up a wet stone and began to pound the flesh, dragging himself as he did this over to the nearest patch of cool water.

The pain was shooting up his leg, and the thigh was swelling alarmingly; but he knew that if he went on pounding the painful flesh he would, sooner or later, drive out the poison with the blood. He must mash the flesh into a pulp, from which the poison could flow out into the water, without, at the same time, breaking any bones; and quickly, before the coma came. He was sweating now. He worked hard for a while, watching the red-staining of the water and then moving over to a cleaner pool when his instinct told him the poison was souring the water.

In a little while it was all over, and he lay on his back gasping, turning his head from side to side with the pain. How fortunate it was that he had told his daughter to stay up near the sun-drenched river! If she should see him like this, he was thinking, she would surely weep her heart out for him, sure that he was dying. Because he knew that she did not really believe in the potency of his yellow-stained toucan bones. He touched the bones again and knew that they had saved him.

The sharp fire was spreading up to his hip, and he was losing the use of his eyes; but this, he knew, was only a matter of resting until his natural resistance should come to his aid. The witch doctors had always told him: *Lie still, and the pain will go.*

He lay gulping in great drafts of air, forcing his breath to come. If he did not keep his chest expanded the muscles would tense up and close his windpipe completely. His eyes were clouding over, and he was terrified that they would burst, as a man's eyes could after a bite from this snake. He blinked his eyes fast. And then the pain swelled into his chest and his lungs, and he screamed out and twisted his body, arching his back up and beginning to flop uncontrollably like a dying fish. He thrashed about in the grass, knowing that there might be other *coralitos* here and that they might attack him. His body curved, and his neck went back till it seemed it must break, and a great sweat drenched him. He found that his fists were clenched, and he could not see where his weapons were. And then the fire inside him leaped up to a peak of anguish, and he shrieked uncontrollably, the tears running down from his eyes, and he threw himself sideways, his arms thrashing in the mud. The pain was more than he could bear.

And, before the sight left his eyes completely, he saw the deep imprint of the jaguar's pads in the wet black soil under his face.

She was shocked when she saw her father. A slim hand flew to her brown face, and her dark eyes were wide.

He was staggering over the edge of the pit, stretching out a hand as though he could not see; she gasped when she saw the mangled foot he was limping on. He was covered from head to foot with black mud, and he looked indeed like one of the demons who lived down there (perhaps, after all, in spite of what the missionaries had told her?). The whole of his left leg was horribly swollen, and it was covered with thousands of tiny red ants. A black swarm of *carapato* ticks was covering his shoulder and swarming up over his neck,

and there was no tobacco to cure the bites they were making.

She ran to him and threw her thin arms around his naked
barrel chest, and she began to cry, and he said, calming her
and secretly pleased at his escape, "It is nothing. I was bitten
by a *coralito,* but the pain has gone now. Only the eyes . . ."

He pushed her away feebly, because the insects were beginning to swarm from his body onto hers, searching for
more blood; she brushed at them disgustedly, rubbing her
hand over his chest and her own shoulder and feeling the
juice of them as they squashed. His eyes were pale and
watery, and frightening to look at. She touched them gently,
and he said, "It is all right; I can see a little. Soon I will be
able to see as well as ever before." He sank down on the
grass, half falling, slipping out of her embrace, and took hold
of his mangled foot and said, "Give me a piece of your skirt,
just a small piece."

She slipped out of her robe, tore a length of the cotton
off, and slipped it around her waist again quickly; she went
over to the fire and scooped some wood ash up onto the ma-
terial and said, "Let me do it. I know how. . . ."

Her thin, delicate fingers moved lightly over the wounds,
rubbing the wood ash into them, and she looked up to ask,
"Perhaps I should suck out the poison?" He shook his head.
"There is not much left. It is in the water down there, where
the devils are. Let them drink it." He was laughing, and she
could not understand why. She crouched over him, putting
on the ash like a wet poultice, and binding it into place with
the rag from her dress.

She said, "You were a long, long time. I was afraid for
you."

He stood up and tried his leg, and said, "You see? The
bone is not broken, only the skin where I hit it with a rock."

It was, in truth, a fearful wound; but he knew that he would not have lived long if he had not done what he had done.

She was trembling for him, and she said suddenly, speaking out more openly than she had ever dared before, "Let us give up this foolish hunt for an animal that has disappeared. Let us go back along the river and count the para trees. Please?" She pleaded with him again, "Please?"

But she knew now why her father, in spite of the terrible state he was in, was so happy. He grinned at her and said, "The animal has not disappeared." He slued around and pointed. "There, where the *arvo' de pao,* the breadfruit tree, is, that is where the animal went. I saw the tracks. I was right. She went over the edge of the water; I told you that was what she had done. She hurt her back legs. I think her back is broken. We will find her easily now."

The child began to cry again. The Indian was astonished. He said, "Do not be foolish. In a short time, before the sun goes down, my eyes will be good again. And then . . . then we will follow the tracks and find the animal."

But it was not until the next day that he fully recovered his sight. When the sun went down and he could see only green darkness and a hazy weaving where his daughter was fussing over him, he remembered the stories he had heard of eyeballs bursting with the poison; it was something to do with the thinning of the blood, but beyond that it had always been one of the terrifying tales of the witch doctors, only half believed. But now . . .

They spent the night shivering under their blankets, listening to the falls, and in the morning Urubelava sat solemnly under a tree with a pulpy plaster of *ajo* leaves bound around his skull, because his head was aching badly.

But when the sun had reached its highest point, he took off the plaster and threw it away, and hobbled to his feet and cut himself a stout stick to help him along, and slung his weapons over his shoulder and went off to find the tracks, now that he knew just where to look. He was enormously pleased with himself that his eyes were better. The mangled foot was a small price to pay.

Under the breadfruit tree he found them. He said, "She is dragging both her rear legs behind her. I do not think she will last very much longer." He held up his own wounded leg, standing there with one foot stuck out incongruously, and roared with laughter and said, "Both of us, you see? Both of us!"

The spoor led off through the forest to the north, toward the pampas. Hobbling on his stick, he followed it. Unhappily, unsmiling even at his laughter, his daughter followed him.

But Bichu's back was not broken.

The agony in the pinched nerves was excruciating at every step, but she forced herself to move, limping along slowly at a broken pace, husbanding her strength, careless of the sounds she made now. She knew that she was strong enough again to fight or run fast if she must. Like Urubelava, she could take advantage of nature's healing powers, and to all the animals of the forest, to all the strong ones, that great reserve would come in times of stress. She was not well; but the strength, the competence, and above all the resolution, were fast returning to her.

The jungle tries an animal's courage; and it also tempers it

The pain in her chest had quite gone, and soon, she knew,

her rear legs would answer her efforts more easily; she had learned this by forcing herself into a faster gait even though it hurt her. From time to time she tucked one foreleg up under her chest and limped along on three legs; and when the pain in her back became too sharp, she put it down again and used all four legs, speeding up when she thought she could safely manage to do so. Sometimes she rested, panting, under a bush, her pink, moist tongue hanging out and making little in-and-out movements; her teeth gleamed white.

The forest was thinning out here and drying up. The vines were less tangled, and as she ran they soon disappeared altogether. There were no more banana trees, nor mangoes, nor breadfruit; and the brilliant orchids gave way to yellow parasites that festooned the dry branches. Even the sounds of the forest disappeared, except for the occasional cry of a parrot that had strayed too far from its own piece of jungle. Instead there was the gentle sound of the wind moving the long grasses; it was a friendly, welcoming whisper. Soon the last of the water was behind her, and ahead lay an immense dry plateau of yellow-brown grass, with a deep-green fringe on its farthest side, many miles away, where the waters began again. And beyond that was the mountain that was her home.

She lay under a bush, recovering her strength, smelling the sweet scent of the waving grasses.

The plateau was another step on the way to her home, to her own territory, the pampas she had so long been waiting to cross.

chapter eleven

When the young girl frowned, her whole face seemed to wrinkle itself up.

The wide eyes narrowed, the heavy black eyebrows arched down, and deep lines that belied her age appeared around the tops of her cheekbones. The innocence of her childhood seemed to leave her, and she was suddenly a grown woman, with a grown woman's responsibilities. And then she would make some childlike gesture, and the illusion of maturity would be gone.

She was frowning now, staring out across the wide pampas and fearing them with the troubling fear of the unknown. They were forest Indians, Urubelava and his daughter; their home was the jungle, which they knew well and were at ease in, and this dry and unknown place was full of dangers for them. There were few trees to hide behind, no rivers at all should they feel thirsty; and above all, there was a strangeness to it that made them both realize just how far they had come from the damp shadows of the tall trees, from the wet banks of green moss and waving ferns, with the mud all around and the ripe vegetation displaying the richness of their customary surroundings.

It was hot and dry and unfriendly here; she hoped desperately that her father would decide not to try to cross it. But it was a forlorn hope. She knew that with each increasing difficulty his pride would force him on, though death itself were waiting to prevent him from completing the task he had set himself.

He was sitting under the last of the trees, using it as an almost symbolic shelter from the parching sun. He looked back once at the jungle, where the rivers were. He held his crutch out at an angle, sticking it out jauntily above his head, and since he had tucked his legs under him instead of squatting on his heels, he was going to stay there and think for a long time before letting her know that he had made up his mind not to fear the pampas.

It was a difficult decision to make, although he had really made it long ago, as soon as he had realized that the jaguar's tracks led toward the green-and-purple hills so far away across the dry grasses. He hoped that the sun would sink before he had finished ruminating, so that during the night he might have a chance to change his mind. She came and squatted beside him, tucking her robe under the backs of her knees and tracing a thin finger across the sand to make crisscross patterns while she waited for him to speak. He showed no signs of wanting to talk, and she said, "The pampas are a dangerous place. There is no water there."

He answered her sharply, because she was telling him something he already knew. "It is not dangerous! It is only . . . unknown. A man is not a man if he is afraid of what he does not know."

She said very quietly, "The para trees grow along the river bank, where there is always water, and food, and shelter."

"I know that, daughter." He wanted to say at once that he had decided to brave the great dangers out there, because if a man changed his mind at the first sign of danger . . . He said, scoffing, "What dangers can there be in the pampas? Nothing lives there."

Very wisely, she said, "And that means that we will die if we try to cross it."

She knew what the danger was. It was not the lack of water. The skin of the jungle Indian was not hardened to the sun, and a few hours out of the forest could burn and blister him, his skin would burst into festering sores, and the flying insects, brought by the smell of seeping blood, would fasten themselves on his body by the millions; if he lay down to rest, the ants would devour him alive. She knew this to be true, because she had heard the tales many times.

But her father was thinking that perhaps she was right; if nothing lived there, surely it was because nothing *could* live? He shook his head slowly, because a decision of such importance had to be his alone.

"No. A man from the village crossed it once, a long time ago, and he came back and said there was nothing there to be afraid of if a man takes water with him. We will fill the pot with water first. It is wise to learn from the experience of others." He pointed at the distant line of trees and said, "And there, where the big trees are, there will be more rivers, just like the ones we have left. There will be food, and water, and shelter."

All hope had left her that he would decide, after all, to go back. She said desperately, "An animal like an *onca*, a jaguar, can cross it quickly, before the sun gets too hot. But for us . . . ?" She gestured at his foot and said, "With your leg, how can we move so fast?"

He said, "The jaguar crossed it, and we are following the

jaguar. Perhaps it will lie down and die before it reaches the other side. Perhaps it is dead already, and it is lying out there no more than a few paces away from us in the long grass. Shall we give up now, when we have come so far? Shall we say we are afraid, and leave a valuable skin a few paces away from us for some braver man to find? The tracks are clear here, and easy to follow. There . . ." he pointed for her to where the dry grass was bent down. "There, only a little while ago, less than one day, that is where the animal entered the grass." Using his stick to point the way, swinging it around in a wide arc, he said, "It came from there, in a straight line, and it is going there, to the other side where the bright green is. That is a stand of banana trees, the nearest river to us now, and that is where the animal is going. That is where we will go too."

"Perhaps the animal will turn around in the tall grass and come back to the river we have left."

"No. Did I not tell you? It has been traveling in a straight line. From the mud where the crocodiles were, to the place where we found the bones of the condor, to the waterfall, and all the way here to the edge of the pampas." He raised a hand and gesticulated broadly and said, "Always in a straight line! It is going to that patch of banana trees over there, and then on up into the mountain, where its home is. I know this! I tell you it is the truth!"

But he did not get to his feet. She knew that he was unable to find an excuse to go no farther that was commensurate with his dignity. She wanted to remind him again of his bad leg, which was still swollen and covered over with dried and caked blood; but she knew that this would only strengthen his determination. She said at last, almost ashamed of herself, "Your daughter is afraid of the pampas."

He put out a hand and touched her and said very gently,

"My daughter is with her father, and there is nothing she need fear."

He still did not stand up. She moved away and made a fire and boiled some coffee from her little bundle, added a few drops of *pinga* to it, and took it across to him. He drank it slowly. He was losing valuable time, but he could not break the habit of regarding time as something of no consequence. He was close on the jaguar's tracks; and there was a worrying idea at the back of his mind that the animal, instead of weakening to the point of death, as he had imagined, was instead gaining strength all the time. He had found the bones of a young tapir back there by the falls, and the tracks of two very small cubs, and he was wondering if the animal were strong enough to join forces with others of its kind. It did not make sense to him that it should, but since anything he did not fully understand disturbed him, he was worried that the *pobru bichu* was now strong enough to kill (if only a very small tapir), and thus find nourishment. The gods that he worshiped, it seemed, had turned against him. Perhaps it was because he had not fully trusted the magic of the yellow bones he had taken down into the pit there where the *coralito* had bitten him. And yet he had survived the deadly snake because of the magic, and he had carefully hung them up in a ceibo tree when he had finished with them in the prescribed manner.

And there was something else. He knew well that all jaguars were not alike, that all snakes, or parrots, or tapirs, or men were not alike. And for this particular *onca* he was beginning to feel a certain restrained respect. It had survived so much, that only strong will could give it the fortitude to overcome so many obstacles. Remembering how he had dragged himself, hand over hand, up the wet slope of the bank out of the pit where the waterfall went, he thought: How could an *onca*, even a strong one, climb up that slippery bank? How could an animal without the use of its back legs manage it? How had it driven itself on without food to revive it, without rest to sustain it? It had been so close to death so many times; there were vultures' bones back there with the dead condor, and the tale they told was very clear. It was all very confusing. . . .

He said aloud, scarcely realizing that he had raised his voice, "We are both strong, both the *onca* and I. But I am stronger."

The pampas were becoming a test. If the animal can cross successfully, he told himself, he would never find it. But if, on the other hand, he were to catch up with it before it reached the other side . . . Time, then, was the important thing, to move now before another moment was lost.

He lay back against his tree and said to his daughter in a loud voice, "We will spend the night here, and in the morning, as soon as it is light, we will enter the pampas and find the animal."

Now that the decision was made, he felt considerably better. All the confusion was shrugged off; tomorrow would be a more felicitous day. He began to pull the leeches off the caked blood on his foot. He had found some tobacco leaves and was chewing them and then rubbing the brown saliva into the wounds; he laughed when the ugly insects squirmed on contact with the juice, and loosened the hold of their tiny teeth so that he could easily flick them away.

His ankle was swollen to three times its normal size, and it was dark purple in color, with patches of greenish-yellow. He inspected it carefully and said, "Good. Soon it will be well again." He hobbled over to the fire and put his foot in the hot ashes, while his daughter carefully, slowly, piled the gray ash all around it. He leaned on his crutch and day-

dreamed while she was working, daydreamed about returning to his village with a fine skin to show what a good man
he was.

Bichu ran till it seemed her lungs would burst.
There was a rhythm now, a rhythm she had not had for a
long time.

She would run on all four legs till the pain that seeped
up into her shoulder became unbearable, and then she
would tuck her right foreleg under her chest and continue
on three legs, changing her gait without stopping; and then,
a little while later, she would touch it to the ground again
and continue once more on four, not stopping until there
was no air left in her gasping body.

The grass was long, well over her head as she forced a way
through it, its tough, wiry stalks flattening before her as she
ran.

In a little while her instinct told her to change her direction radically, and she made a wide sweep to one side,
doubling back almost on her own tracks, and she pulled up
sharply at a outcrop of flat red rock, crossing it slowly at a
walk and examining the ground carefully to see which was
the best place to enter the grass again. She decided that she
would continue the circle, as though she were returning to
the jungle she had left; and soon she swung back again on
her original course toward the great patch of banana trees
where the other river was.

She found a huge umbrella tree that stood in the middle
of the plain, and for a moment or two she sniffed around
at its base to see if there were any water there; there was

none, and she climbed up into its branches to rest, flattening herself along one of the great branches and backing in among the leaves until she was invisible. She gripped the bark with her claws, and let her tongue hang out in the fresh breeze, and licked at her dry muzzle, and tried not to notice the pain as she turned her head sharply from this side to that, searching out the far forest and seeing how much closer it was now. She sniffed at the air constantly.

She would have liked to sleep for just a little while; but this was not the time or the place. There was little danger for her in the pampas, but neither was there cover. The wind was slight, and it was behind her, and there was satisfaction in knowing that it bore no scent of the dreadful enemies who had been following her for so long.

She flattened her muzzle against the branch and stared out across the grass, letting the strength come back to her. The sun was directly overhead; it was a bad time to move.

And then she felt the prickling of fear at the back of her neck. There was a new scent coming to her from behind and to one side. Her head moved up quickly, her sharp eyes fixed in the precise direction of the odor. Far, very far away, there were black patches moving against the yellow grass; a little closer to her, the grass itself was moving slightly. She heard the barking of dogs.

She slipped down from her high perch and raced through the grass, moving like spotted lightning in her terror, both forelegs reaching out, and the rear legs pumping the ground away from her as she sped over it as fast as she had ever run. When the pains came she was expecting them, ready for them. She bit through her tongue in the anguish, but she did not check her speed.

The dogs had taken the scent of her tracks.

There were ten or twelve of them, evil, scraggy, mangy beasts that lived in perpetual hunger. Their hair was long and dark brown and matted with dirt and their snouts were sharp-pointed, and their tick-infested ears lay back against their flattened heads. The leader pulled up short on his strong front legs, threw back his head, and howled loudly, the sound traveling far over the grass; the others got away from him, racing fast along the track, not dropping their heads, but following the strong scent at head height.

The howl was a call, for these were no ordinary dogs. Lusting for blood, they were trained to track for their masters, trained to kill or maim. And so the leader rested back on his haunches and wailed his terrible cry; and he waited till he heard the sound of galloping hooves, and then, as the master rode up very fast, he raced off again after the other dogs, his white teeth already snapping. He would bring them back into line and take the lead; he would have to kill one or two of them before they obeyed him, he knew. But he did not wait for his master to drop quickly and lightly off the horse; he raced on along the tunnel in the grass that the others had made. His yowling had stopped, and now he was barking as fiercely as the others, racing to catch up with them and to hunt the quarry down.

The man was slim, and wiry, and dark, with a khaki shirt and baggy pants that did not hide the whipcord muscles. He threw himself off his horse without checking his movement, and was on his hands and knees, looking at the tracks, and straightening up again all in one motion, turning back his head and yelling, his white teeth gleaming: *"Onca! Onca! Onca!"*

He did not stop for his call to be answered. But with an easy leap he was back on his broad saddle and whipping the tiny pony into action.

The others raced up to him as he speeded off, laughing and yelling and swinging their bolas wildly; there were four of them altogether, gauchos out hunting rheas, the short, two-toed ostriches of the plains; though for more than a week's travel they had seen not a single one, only a clutch of eighteen bright-green eggs which they had carefully hidden, to be picked up on the return journey to their nomadic homes.

They moved on their horses with an effortless ease, swinging their whips from side to side, barreling down the parting in the grass that showed where the dogs and the jaguar had gone; one of them was even picking his teeth with the point of a sharp knife as he rode. They rode, unstopping, past the dead body of one of the dogs that the leader had quickly killed in his demand for mastery. They gave it no more than a cursory glance, for dogs were easy to come by and the leader would do all the training that was necessary. The jaguar was more important; it was a useful skin, and more, it was good sport to run down and kill the fastest animal in the jungle or on the plains.

They could hear the dogs' barking much louder now, and the note of it had changed: they were catching up. One of the men signaled, and the other three turned their horses and spread out from the single file, forming a wide arc. They had slipped their bolas over the pommels of their saddles; now they slipped them free again and began limbering up by winding them around and around their heads. The dogs would attack the jaguar and force it to stand and fight; and then they would hurl their bolas to bring it to its knees; a slash with a knife across the throat, and all the sport would be over.

It was almost too easy.

Bichu's lungs were bursting.

There was no more tall grass. Here it was much shorter, and easier to run through. There was a mile or so to cover before she reached the shelter of the forest, but the ground was already damp under her feet with the approaching marshes.

Her head was flat, and so was her tail, both in line with her extended body, and her eyes were moving from side to side rapidly to keep an eye on the two foremost dogs. There was one to each side of her, gaining on her just a little. Farther behind, she could hear the shouts of the men and the sound of their horses' hooves. Her pace had slackened, and now she was filled with terror. The dogs were moving faster and easier than she was; her breathing was labored, and there was a rasping sound coming from her throat; she was beginning to spit blood again; the wound reopened in her belly. The pain all down her side and in her ribs was agonizing, but she would not stop; the jungle that meant safety was too close, and she drove herself harder than she had ever driven herself before.

The dog on her right (the bad side) had slowed to a lope, and she turned in that direction, hoping to cut across his front and lose the dog to her left. And then, suddenly, the leader was there, in front of her, and she saw too late that she had been tricked. It was the pack against the individual; and the pack was working with a mind of its own. The leader had made a wide circle and was hurtling toward her, head on. His ears lay flat, his eyes were bright, and his teeth were shining. The great solid chest was broad and heavy, and there was saliva slobbering out of the ugly mouth. He was coming straight at her, his teeth bared to rip into her, his muscles rippling as smoothly as her own.

She did not check herself. She stretched out farther with her front legs and sprang, and in midair the two animals collided. There was a blurred, bounding movement, and Bichu was on her back with sharp teeth sunk deep into her neck. She tucked her rear legs under her and hooked out with them both at once. The steel claws ripped into the dog's belly and tore it wide open, throwing the screaming body away from her as she wrenched herself sideways and onto her feet again. Teeth snapped at her haunches, and she increased her pace, and then the water was there and she was swimming in it, up to her neck, with her forelegs pumping fast, with no ground underneath her. She could hear the dogs splashing clumsily into the water, but she was a better swimmer than they were, and she was gaining on them. She heard the splashing of the horses' hooves and the shouts of the gauchos, and something whistled around her head and made her wince.

On the other bank she streaked up the slope of a fallen tree, reaching the high branches and leaping without thought across a great gap of open air into the branches of a cedar that overhung the broken rocks she had glimpsed and recognized as safety.

Her long, smooth body flew like a bird through the branches, and then she was on the ground again, falling hard but with firm, scattered rocks under her feet. More water then, and the deep shadows of overhanging ferns and tangled lianas, and then she was worming her way under a heavy log, close to the ground, where a rivulet was seeping under the rocks, and out on the other side to the shining, friendly boulders. She did not stop. She sped up the steep slope of the rocks, red, and gray, and shining white, up and up and over everything, not stopping to look back at the danger behind her. Another tree, a long branch that crossed a deep gully, a patch of stinking mire, a clump of bamboo to plow through, a deep pool to swim across, more rocks to climb, a steep slope that led her higher and higher . . . Only when she reached the top did she stop and turn; behind her there was nothing.

She could hear the savage barking of the dogs as they lost the trail; she could hear, not knowing what it was, the jeering and the laughter of the gauchos; she could hear the screams of a dying horse that had fallen on the broken ground. The sounds began to fade.

She stood poised on the red sandstone outcrop that towered up over the rivers and the marsh below, her long tail extended and gently moving from side to side, her round head steady, her chest expanding and contracting rapidly, her four legs firm and rooted in the ground. She trembled a little, and she saw the dark shadows that were the horses moving away, moving fast, with the ugly, vicious dogs—angered and snarling at each other—moving away behind them. In the distance she could see the bloodied body of the one she had killed; two of the others were already tearing the carcass to pieces, and the rest came up and began to fight each other for the meat.

Bichu turned away. There was a rending sickness in her stomach. She dropped down on her belly and vomited, and then she began to move away.

Her legs were uncoordinated, her movements erratic and unsteady. She coughed out some blood, but soon she found a pool of fresh water and drank deeply; she moved off into the shade of the tall banana trees, stumbled deep into their cool shadows, and fell over onto her side the moment she tried to lie down. Her head was jerking in little shudders, and when she tried to still them she found she had almost no control at all. There was a dull pain at the back of her neck. She could not see the jagged hole sharp teeth had torn when the dog had tried to break her neck with the first savage bite, but the white bone of her spine was showing, half covered with clotting blood; a piece of her skin was flapping loosely behind her ear. To ease the pain, she tried to roll over onto her back, but she could not. She struggled and then let the lassitude take her; and soon she was restlessly half asleep.

The broad leaves of the banana trees cast dappled shadows over the yellow of her fur and the dark, broken-horseshoe spots. Some birds were calling loudly in the branches. An immense swarm of butterflies flew overhead and blocked out the light of the sun. She was vaguely aware of the thundering sound of a herd of peccaries, a big one, galloping past nearby, and she smelled the strong scent of them; but she could not muster the energy even to think of food. She awakened, and slept again, and came once more to a startled consciousness that was filled with pain, and slept again. . . .

And in her sleep she imagined that she was surrounded with fresh, rich food; but the food changed itself to the bloated carcass of the dead dog, and other dogs were fighting her for it, tearing painfully at her intestines and dragging them out all over the grass; and she awakened suddenly, and found herself snarling at nothing.

Uneasily, she settled back to sleep again.

chapter twelve

Urubelava too was trembling.

In all his life he had never been so frightened. He lay flat on his face in the pampas grass, the long grass that towered high over his head even when he was walking, and he held his daughter's wrist tightly to comfort her and let her know that he was always beside her when danger was threatening. He was praying quietly to his gods, the gods who were so mysterious that even their names were not known to him. But there was one god whose particular province was the sun and the wind and the water, and he was thinking silently, over and over again, *Let the wind not change, let the wind not change. . . .*

That wind was bringing him the scent of horses and of dogs and of the dreaded gauchos.

He could hear them, talking and laughing cheerfully in their strange Portuguese and occasionally yelling insults at their hounds; the horses were walking quietly, and they were only a few hundred paces away from him, over to one side, where the animal had left the tracks that swung back toward the river he had left and had almost convinced him that she was returning to the jungle to the south.

He lay so still that he was not even breathing. This was something he had learned to do many years before when he was a small boy and raiders would sometimes descend on the village in their search for women. He would hide, in those distant days, quite close to the compound so that he would know when the raiders had left, and he would hold his breath for an incredible length of time, immobile as a wooden statue; it was something all the hill Indians could do.

Even his eyes did not move; they were fixed on the back of his daughter's head. Fear had petrified her too, so there was no danger of her moving either.

He knew exactly what they were doing and why they were there; it was common knowledge in his village. Someone had told them: *Go into the deep country and kill all the Indians you find there.* This was something the men in the village whispered about, knowing only that there were strangers who thought that they, the Indians, represented a danger and must be destroyed.

A danger to whom? To what? There were terrible tales told at night, in quiet voices by the fires, of groups of helpless Indians driven off into the jungle and slaughtered, with great cruelty and much laughter; and they had never been able to learn why. The gauchos, the elders said, were even worse than the *desatitos,* who wanted only slaves to pick wild rubber for them or women to give them sons; and this, at least, was understandable. But the gauchos . . . With them it was a matter of killing for sport and without reason.

With great dignity and patience, one of the elders had told Urubelava, many years ago, "If you see or hear a man on a horse, on the grasses of the pampas, this is a gaucho.

He will chase you with his horse and will throw stones that are tied together with leather thongs, and the thongs will bind your legs stronger than a man can bind them. And then he will trample you with his horse, or kill you with his knife, or drag you behind him at the gallop until you are dead. So when you see or hear this man, then you must hide yourself as you would from a *desatito*, until all the danger is gone, and then you will hide for a long time more, and you must always remember this."

And Urubelava had remembered. He lay now with a hand on his daughter's arm, praying that the wind would not take their scent to the horsemen.

The ants of the grasses had found the blood on his leg; there were thousands of them swarming over him; still, he did not move a hair's breadth or allow a muscle to shudder.

They passed him by so close that he could smell not only their sour sweat but also the *feijao*, the mixture of rice and beans they carried in their saddlebags. But the wind did not change, and the sounds grew fainter and fainter, and still Urubelava and his daughter did not move. They lay still for many hours, until the darkness came; once, when he felt the trifling of a movement in his daughter's arm, he gripped her so tightly that she would have cried out if she had not been so terrified.

When it was dark he got slowly to his feet and listened, and smelled the air, and shuddered once, and said, "We will hurry forward, even though it is night, and we will reach the waters, where there is safety from these evil men."

She was still too frightened to answer him; and she kept up with him easily as he ran at a fast, easy lope, his bad leg forgotten in the urgency of the moment, not stopping until they reached the jungle on the other side.

There was light in the east now, and they quickly found

a hiding place among the bushes, curling themselves up in a hole in the ground like animals, not speaking, not even looking at each other until the last trace of the fear had faded.

Here, with the friendly shadows all around them, it did not really take long. By the time the sun was halfway up the blue sky, Urubelava was beginning to grin slowly to himself; and soon he was laughing outright at the danger they had so successfully overcome together. He said, "You see, the gods are on the side of a brave man; they come to help me every time I am in trouble."

He cut himself a new crutch, because he had left the old one lying in the long grass in his haste to get away as soon as darkness fell; all the danger of the unknown pampas was behind them, and they were at home once again in the jungle, where the shadows gave cover in time of danger. He walked for a long time in the morning sunlight up and down the edge of the forest (keeping the grassy plain in sight but never venturing too far from the trees); and at last he found what he was looking for.

He clicked his tongue noisily and said, "The animal is running now, very fast; come and look at her tracks." When his daughter dutifully came over to stare at the ground, he said, teaching her to read the signs, "Do you see? The gauchos were chasing her. They did not catch her, but the dogs . . . They were close behind her, and there is blood; she has been hurt again. I think one of the dogs bit her." He moved across the moss and said, "You see, even here they were close behind her, but the big dog is not there anymore." He stared out across the plain and said, "They came from there, chasing her, the gauchos on the horses, and when they came to the forest they turned back, because the gauchos cannot live in the forest." He found this very funny and laughed away his fear of them. "Can you believe that a man cannot live in the forest?"

Her eyes were bright, and he said, "It is because of the horses. Horses move very fast, and when they run, they cannot stop if there is a tree in their way, and so . . . Bang!" He made a broad gesture to show her how a horse at speed would collide with a tree, and she laughed now, and said through the laughter, "Like Akuriba, when he walks in his sleep."

He stopped laughing abruptly, and his face was puzzled. He said slowly, "How can a wounded *onca* outrun the horses of the gauchos? How can it outrun their dogs? I tell you, daughter, this is not an ordinary jaguar." He badly wanted to go back into the pampas a little way, just far enough to read the signs on the ground and see where the *onca* had first taken the scent of the dogs, to learn what had happened, if truly she had killed one of them, the big one with the twisted toe on his left front foot; but he was afraid, and so he shrugged off the idea.

But there was a gap in his knowledge now. For many, many days he had followed the tracks, and he had known every single thing that had happened, except this. He said again, worrying about it: "There is blood, fresh blood; she was bitten. One of the dogs, perhaps more of them, bit her, so how could she escape? An *onca* cannot fight a pack of dogs and survive. But she did. Her tracks tell me that she did."

Moving deeper into the jungle, he soon found the place where Bichu had found her first cover. He found the sloping, half-fallen tree with her claw marks on it and had to cast around for a long time till he saw where she had left the trees and came back to the ground again. And then they climbed the high bluff of red stone and stood together on the top, looking back on the pampas valley just as she had done; even from up here it looked a frightening place, and he could not help murmuring, "You see? That is where we crossed, a long, long journey. They will be proud of us in the village when I tell them."

Close around their feet were the pad marks. A tiny rivulet was running here, the white water dropping in a thin stream down to the rocks below; it made a pleasant, homely sound. He dropped to his knees and looked at the earth and said gruffly, "It is clay. We will make a pot for food."

He did not want to elaborate. When he had run from the grass in his fright, he had left the pot as well as his crutch behind. This was his daughter's responsibility, not his. But with the crutch lost as well, how could he blame her for it? He chose to treat it as a trifle, although the pot was of white-enameled metal that was chipped in only one or two places and had been carried by them for longer than he could remember. She too chose to say nothing. Since her father had not beaten her for losing it, he could not really mind too much.

She took his long knife and cut a sharp stick, and dug up some clay with it, and made a hole in the ground close to the water, and dropped in the dry clay and scooped water over it; and then, while he strung his bow and checked the alignment of his arrows again, she trampled the wet clay with her bare feet until it was of just the right consistency; then she took the heavy dollop over to her father.

He took it from her and thumped at it, nodding his head. And he shaped it slowly and carefully into the form of a deep bowl, using his short, stubby fingers with great delicacy, and by the time the shape was right she had built the fire, and they sat down together and waited for the embers to burn down. Soon he placed the clay pot in the hot ashes, and piled more ash inside it, and left her to keep an eye on the process while he went off to hunt for food..

There was fish in the scattered waters here, but he craved other meat, and he prowled the jungle to see what it had to offer. He found a dead anaconda, more than fifteen paces long, that had been cut to ribbons just a little while ago, and he examined the signs excitedly. He saw that two large peccaries, out of a herd of fifty or more, had attacked the snake, leaping on it with their four sharp-hooved feet close together just when the snake's strike had brought it flat along the ground. Delighted with his fortune, he followed the spoor, and soon he caught up with the herd. There were far more of the peccaries than he could count, but he moved silently to the side of the herd and searched out the one he wanted, and shot it three times, very quickly, with three arrows into the neck. He waited cautiously till the others had passed on, and then he slung the carcass over his strong shoulders and carried it back to his daughter.

She built another fire while he skinned it, and tossed great hunks of meat onto the flaming roots, and they ate until their stomachs were bloated. He cut the fresh hide into long strips to make a rope, and she wove some of it into a sling for the clay pot that was now nearly ready. He cut a wide patch of leather, wet it, bound it around his ankle, and threw away his new crutch. The tightening binding was even better than a stick.

And, a little while before midday, they were once more following the tracks of the *pobru bichu*.

The fire was part of the forest pattern.

In this great, rich land that spread so far to the distant horizons, with no sign of any living thing, there were secrets that moved, hiding, from tree to bush, from fern to tangled thicket; and the secrets were the animals and the scattered Indians.

Of the Indians, there were so very few. Hiding was part of the fabric of their lives, and a man could walk through a thousand miles of jungle and never see one of them, although he might, if he were very perceptive, become aware that somewhere in the thick forest close by there were hidden creatures who were watching him, creeping from shadow to shadow, their painted bodies blending perfectly with the jungle colors.

Or he would see the smoke of their fires.

They would travel through the day, and at night they would light a small fire and sit around it whispering together or staring into the flames in silence, squatting on their heels and smoking their pipes. Their faces would be solemn, and weary, and very sad. These were the widely scattered remnants of a Stone Age culture that was slowly being bulldozed out of existence.

At dawn they would move on again, leaving their fires behind them, moving a few more miles to another part of this limitless land, and settling down once more around the nightly fire. Sometimes there would be other lonely Indians, just as well hidden, who would watch the receding fires carefully each night, the wisps of blue smoke getting farther and farther away, and moving out of hiding only when the number of fires matched the number of fingers on a hand and it was safe to move again. One would never know who the other had been, or where he came from, or where he was going.

The fires, when the Indians had moved on, would smolder and spread a little, and reach the water or the damp moss, and slowly extinguish themselves. Or sometimes there would be dry grasses nearby that would burst into flame, or a dead tree would fall across the embers, or a wind would spring up and blow sparks. And then it seemed as though the whole forest, wet or dry, would leap into flame. A thousand, ten thousand, a hundred thousand acres or more would suddenly be on fire, the flames spreading quickly because the forest was so dense and tightly packed with oil-rich vines, or dead branches, or fresh green wood.

But it never seemed to matter. What if a hundred miles of forest burned? A man could not count the thousands of miles that remained untouched, on the other side of the many winding rivers.

The silent, hidden men who started them would have moved on, unknown and anonymous, soon to disappear themselves. For those of the animals who could swim, there was safety in the waters; but the others could only race in panic from water barrier to water barrier, within an ever-decreasing space, where the burning trees were crashing down around them to bring their struggles for survival finally to a close.

Bichu was instantly awake when she smelled the smoke; this was one of the dangers that she knew well.

Her head came up sharply, her eyes alert, her ears pricked back to listen for the sharp, crackling sound; it was terribly close. She heard, and saw, an antelope crashing through the bush a little to one side of her, and she looked where it had come from and saw the dark smudge that told her where the fire was starting. She leaped to her feet, and a strangled cry came from her throat as the pains hit her; but she began to run, forcing her legs to move, heading in the direction the antelope had taken.

She ran fast till she came to a stream, and she plunged in up to her head, feeling the bite of the cold water on her lacerated neck. The weeds closed tightly around her, parting for her as she moved, comforting her with their cool touch as she swam slowly, in a circle, taking her time and watching the smoke and the wind. It was easier for her to swim than to run; the pains in her body were easier to bear.

A flock of red and blue *papagaios*, screeching, flew over her head, fast, and the trees were alive with the racing monkeys, leaping from branch to branch, reaching out with hands and prehensile tails. She turned to one side, following the course of the running stream, but the smoke grew thicker here, the scent of burning richer; she began to see flames, and she turned back and fought the current strongly.

A screaming deer, its body blackened, plunged into the water close beside her, and rolled over with terrified eyes, and died. A boa plopped noisily down from a tree above her. Two huge otters, more than half her own length, were swimming alongside her, overtaking her and disappearing under the water.

The forest all around her was full of movement, of racing animals, all heading in panic for the far bank. She swam strongly past them, swimming upstream until a giant castanea tree, its branches heavy with great globular clusters of Brazil nuts, seemed to burst into flames and toppled into the water directly ahead of her; she heard the hissing of the steam, and it alarmed her almost as much as the great heat of the air now. She ducked her head under the water, and when she came up again the heat was insupportable. She turned and swam back.

The whole of the bank she had left behind her was in flames now, and she could hear the screams of a burning armadillo as it tried to force a way out of its burrow, blocked by flaming logs. A huge red carpet of grasshoppers, each one as large as a sparrow, was crawling across the surface of the water, the dead serving to form a flexible bridge of writhing bodies; there were hundreds of thousands of them, a gigantic column that at one end disappeared into the flames, and at the other was desperately striving to reach the opposite bank.

The water itself seemed to be on fire, blackened with burning branches; and flaming twigs were being carried on the strong wind to the other side; already some of the tree-tops there were catching fire.

She scrambled heavily up the bank. There was no longer safety in this stretch of water; the air was too hot to breathe, and she raced on, gasping, driving herself along and joining the monkeys and the deer and the peccaries and the running, flightless birds. She was startled when another jaguar raced past her and was gone as quickly as it had appeared; an ocelot was carrying a small cub in its mouth as it shot across her path and was gone. Over the cries of the animals, the roar of the hot wind was terrifying. There was the strong scent of burning meat.

A flaming branch fell on her and singed her coat, and she twisted from under it and sped on. She stumbled into a deep gully, falling over herself in her speed and crashing through the ferns to the bottom. There was water here, and steep sides of gray water-washed rock, and a loud bubbling sound that told her the water was falling close by. She turned toward the sound and swam fast, and soon the water was swirling around her, and above her a large pool was gushing down onto the rocks, falling a dozen feet or more and sending up a thick spray all around her. She crawled out onto the wet rocks, under the fall, and fell flat on her belly, her four legs outstretched, gulping in great mouthfuls of fresh, damp air.

She knew that here she was safe, and so she stayed. The roar of the burning jungle was loud in her ears, but here the falling water gave off a friendly sound, and the wide spray cooled the hot air, and the wet rocks gave shelter. Here she would wait till the fire had burned itself out. She would wait longer for the forest floor to cool off; and then she would struggle on, on her way to the mountains.

She crawled to her feet and moved around slowly, testing her strength, smelling out the old scents and looking for new ones, checking to make sure that there was nothing here that could be a danger to her. She stared for a while at a group of sweet-scented parasites that had patterned themselves strangely along an overhanging branch; there were red, and yellow, and dark purple flowers in three separate groups, three different parasitic growths that were slowly draining the life out of the great softwood mahogany they had fastened themselves to. The colors were brilliant and startling, bright as parrot feathers or butterfly wings, and they swayed gently in the wind, washed by the falling spray.

When she was quite sure that there was no danger in this shining, rocky recess, Bichu lay down to rest on the red-gray granite. To rest, and to wait.

Urubelava too had found water.

He had moved away from the fire quite casually at first, knowing that there were always fires and that they did no harm if a man simply kept away from them.

But when the wind veered around a trifle, he stared at the blackening sky for a while, and then slung his arrows and his bow over his shoulder, and said to his daughter, "Take your things; we must run."

The girl picked up her bundle and slung the new pot round her neck, and at an easy lope they ran across the direction the fire was taking. He called out to her, pointing, "There, by the chicle trees; there is deep water there." He had never been to this place before, but finding water was no problem to him. He could look at a distant stand of trees, darker or lighter in their green than the others, and say with assurance, *There; there is deep water.* Or again, *There will be too much mud there; to the other side is better.* Or even, *There is salt in the water over there; it is not good.*

They ran steadily toward the big sapote trees that were sometimes tapped for chicle gum; and just as he had said, there was a deep pool here, with high rocks around it, and tiny rivulets draining into it from a dozen different directions. He plunged in and headed for the gray-red rocks of smooth granite clustered together in the center, like some ancient temple that stood alone and regal, surrounded by its own wide moat, looking back over his shoulder to see that his daughter was following him. She had fallen back a little to tie her bundle onto her head, and when he called out impatiently, "You must hurry now," she nodded and struck out strongly toward him, her thin arms slicing through the water easily and effortlessly.

She joined him, squatting on the granite slabs half underwater, while he carefully wiped his bow with his hand and laid it out on a smooth rock to dry before the water should penetrate the wood and cause it to warp. He shook his head when he saw the state of his arrows and set about straightening them immediately.

She unwrapped her wet bundle and brought out a large piece of cooked meat that she had saved from the peccary they had roasted, and showed it to him, her eyes excited while she waited for his approval. He had not told her to bring it; it was her own idea. He laughed at her and said, "Why did you carry meat? There is always meat."

She gestured around her at the burning forest and said, "Here? Here we will find meat? It is all cooked too much."

He thought it was a very funny statement, and he laughed over it for a long time. He reached out with his *facao* and sliced the meat into two pieces and started chewing on one of them even though he was not hungry; he wanted to show her that she had indeed had a good idea.

They ate silently, watching the flaming forest all around them. The sweat was pouring off their brown bodies in the burning air, and from time to time sparks would shower down on them and send them scurrying momentarily under the water, to emerge laughing again at the huge joke of their near danger.

The pool was large, five or six hundred paces across, and though the air was hot it was breathable. She finished her meat and dived down to find out how deep the pool was,

and came up, astonished, to tell her father that it was so
deep she could not find the bottom.

He nodded. "I told you. Deep water by the chicle trees—
it is always so." It was a matter of course that he should be
right. He could hear falling water nearby, to one side, and
he pointed and said, "Swim over there and see if we are in a
pool or a river." She wiped the water out of her eyes and
nodded, and when she had swum away with strong, silent
strokes, he chewed at the meat he did not really want, slicing it off at his mouth and shouting after her, "It is good
that you brought the meat."

When she came back, she said delightedly, "There are
red and yellow and purple flowers down there, on the branch
of a mahogany tree. They look like the feathers of *papagaios*."

"A pool. Or a river?"

"A pool. The water falls the height of two men into
another pool. That is where the bright flowers are. They are
like the wings of butterflies."

He nodded.

She climbed up out of the water, and he lay on his back
on the wet rocks and let her scrape the insects off his festering foot.

She stripped off the leather bindings and soaked them in
water and replaced them, noticing that the purple patches
were getting smaller. She pointed out a patch of gray-green-
yellow above the ankle, and he sat up to examine it carefully,
and said finally, "It is nothing. Soon it will be well again.
Not too tight with the leather; it is wet."

He rolled over on his side while she worked, to reach for
the bundle she had laid out to dry, and found that the little
pinga bottle was nearly empty and that there were hardly
any coffee beans left. He grunted. His daughter looked at

him quickly with inquiring eyes and asked, "You want coffee?" She gestured at the bare wet rocks and said, "But how will I make a fire?"

The roar of the burning forest across the water was not enough to drown out his laughter. His leathery face wrinkled up, his teeth shone white, his body rocked from side to side as his laughter sounded in great belly-shaking guffaws; the tears fell down his shining, sweating cheeks.

And watching him, she thought she had never before been so very happy. When he was wiping away the tears, she asked, "And now?"

He shrugged. "We will wait here till the fire has burned itself out."

"And then?"

He hesitated. At last he said, "Then we will try to find the tracks again. After the fire it will not be easy." He pointed and said, "We left them back there, close by the *quinaquina* trees. We will go back there, and we will follow them."

Her heart was very heavy. She said sadly, "Perhaps, in the fire, the *pobru bichu* died."

He shook his head, quite sure of himself. He said gravely, "No. Not this animal. Nothing will kill this animal, except . . ." He turned away from her, not wanting to look at her eyes. He ended, "This animal . . . only a great hunter will kill her."

chapter thirteen

Each was unaware of the other's proximity.

They had dogged each other's tracks for a long time; sometimes they had been close together, sometimes far apart. It was skill and it was chance that kept them chained together. Now the hunt was coming to an end; and neither of them knew how close were the hunter and the hunted.

The stream-fed pool that poured its surplus waters down onto the lower level was open now to the light of the evening. The great canopy of dark-green branches that had fringed it, the huge limbs almost meeting and cutting out the sun completely, had burned away, except where the rising spray had saved them. The lianas trailed forlornly, deprived of their support. Soon they would find the ground with their fingers and start new roots, and the greenery would spring up again; first the vines, and then the shooting saplings, and then the great ferns, till at last the forest here was once more just as it used to be.

It would take time, and underneath the still-warm ashes, the dead bodies of a thousand animals were already rotting down into the nourishment that the jungle craved for its continued growth. There was no true death here, only a change of form.

At this moment, no doubt, there were hundreds of other fires burning in other parts of the forest. But here the life cycle was already beginning again; by tomorrow the first new green shoots would already be appearing through the gray embers.

On the level granite slabs, half submerged, Urubelava and his daughter climbed to the topmost rock and looked over the shining expanse of the pool. It was strange, so deep in the forest, to see the evening sunlight reflected red on the waters; now that the green canopy had gone, the brilliant colors of the sky were copied below them, and the water, which would have been green and darkening now, was shining in reds and yellows and shimmering copper; the black reflections of burned-out trees, still standing, were mirrored starkly.

The picture was strangely perfect, and they stared at it for a while in silence, knowing that this was a rare sight for them to enjoy; but when they lifted their eyes, there was only a dark-gray desolation all around them, as far as they could see.

Urubelava muttered abruptly, "We must leave this place. It is not good." He wanted to find the friendly greens of the leaves he was accustomed to. In the desolation there was no danger; but it seemed now almost as terrible as the pampas. He wondered idly if the plain had burned too, and shuddered to think what would have happened to them had the fire started when they were out in the middle of the pampas; the flames in the dry grasses spread so fast that neither man nor animal could ever hope to outrun them.

He examined, first, the straightness of his arrows, finding them satisfactory and handing them one by one to his daughter to hold while he sighted down the others, holding them up to the sky and twirling them slowly. The two blunt-headed shafts he carried for stunning birds if he wanted to catch one alive were both warped and he twisted off the carefully carved heads and discarded the rest. The fletching on two of the others had come loose, and soon he would have to make some pitch to stick them on again. He examined minutely the blade of his knife and spent a long time honing it on the granite that had served him as a resting place.

He tapped the new pot lightly with his knuckles to make sure it had not been cracked. He found the flat piece of susu bark tucked away in the bundle, the bark he had brought with him on which to mark down the number of the para trees that had first caused him to leave his village; he grunted at it and put it away again. He loosened the leather binding around his foot a little, and then, on reflection, he took it off altogether and said to his daughter, "We have a long way to walk through the ashes; they will make the foot well."

He was moving easily now on the bad foot, scarcely limping at all; the sharp pains had gone, and there was only a dull ache, which was easy to get used to. He looked over toward the little weir, and asked, "When you saw the bright-colored flowers, was there also liana?"

She nodded. "Hanging down in the water, a lot of liana."

"Pack up the bundle; we will move soon. But first, I will get liana, and we will have some fish."

He tucked his knife into the string around his waist, slipped into the water, and swam to the edge of the little falls, checking himself easily on the rocks there, and looked down for the liana. He would cut a few strands, crush them to a pulp, and find some still water to soak them in. The poisonous juice from the vines would blind the fish and bring them to the surface, where they would be easy to catch with his bare hands. He climbed down over the rocks, slashed a handful of the thin, trailing branches, and looked around him at the curtain of water that fell from the pool above. He had an idea then, and carefully cut a few of the red, yellow, and purple flowers from the mahogany branch, and laughed quietly to himself as he stuck them in his hair; it would be a happy surprise for his daughter. He began to climb back.

And, as he pulled himself up, hand over hand, his splayed feet firm on the slippery stones, Bichu was watching him.

There was no scent. The falling water and the spray washed away all the odors, and when she saw, startled, the brown shadow of his movement, she froze. Her eyes were sharp, and when she saw it was only a shadow, she slipped very quickly a trifle deeper under the rocks that were hiding her. Silently, she immersed her body in the water, with only her head above it, the splashing water falling in a curtain to shield her, the granite cold and hard against her ear. He was no more than a few feet away, looking up, reaching up, moving up.

If he could have seen her now he would have seen nothing more than the yellow-brown bullet head, half immersed, with one unblinking eye staring at him and watching every move that he made. The rest of her body was underwater,

and the camouflage of the rocks was perfect. She did not
move, not even when a water snake swam slowly past her,
disturbed in its nest by the warm proximity of her body.

She saw him then, quite clearly. The shadow took on form
and became a man, and he was reaching out for the rocks
above his head, his arms outspread. She could have reached
out with a foreleg and slashed at his vulnerable belly, ripping it open with a single stroke; but she did not move. And,
in a moment, he was gone.

Bichu kept still for a very long time.

He pounded the lianas into a pulp and let them
trail in the water, and soon the fish were coming up to the
surface, blinded, flapping their silvery bodies in bewilder-
ment. Together they reached out and collected half a dozen
or so, and Urubelava swam with them to the shore and
placed them in a pile over some still-hot ashes from the forest
fire; then he swam back to the sanctuary to wait.

She asked, "It is still too hot to walk on?"

He nodded. "In a little while."

She looked across at the yellow sun, low on the horizon
where the purple hills were. "Then we will sleep here again
tonight?"

He scratched his chin and thought about this for a long
time, knowing it would soon be dark and not knowing how
far they would have to go before the gray of the fire would
have been left behind them; there was always, too, the
danger that it would suddenly start again. He nodded at
last and said gravely, "It would be better. When we have
eaten the fish, we will sleep. And as soon as the sun comes up

we will move away from here." She wanted to ask which way, but she was afraid to.

He climbed up to the top of the wet rocks and stood there looking to the north. Through the blackened branches he could see the greens farther away, where yet another of the rivers had stopped the fire; it was a long way off. To his left and to his right there were nothing but scarred and smoldering trees, and behind him, where the pampas lay, he could just see the yellow-green of the grass. He slithered down to her and said, "The land we are on is long and thin, like a man's tongue. The fire went a long way there . . . and there . . . and it was stopped a little way ahead of us. I think if we go now, we can reach the green again before it is dark."

He did not like to tell her that he was afraid of the ravaged shadows around them; he craved living things around him, and here there was only death; it made him shudder. And most of all he wanted to continue the hunt, because in the hunt there was life, and there was his mastery of it. It was essential that he escape at once from this dreadful place. He said again, "We will not stay here. We will move on."

She looked quickly at the ashes across the water. "But the fish to eat?"

He said, "We ate today. We will go. Now."

Obediently she strapped her bundle on her head, slung the cooking pot around her neck, and followed him into the water. She knew that his trembling was a reflection of his urge toward the jaguar.

They walked until the sun had gone down and it was nearly dark, and when they reached the river and waded across it, cooling their feet in the water after the hot forest floor, they found themselves on a steeply sloping swell of sweet-smelling thyme and wild mint. A huge passiflora vine stretched over the bank for as far as they could see, a single plant that bore more than a hundred ripe fruit. There was a tall cherimoya, too, and a million insects were buzzing around the fallen fruit.

He said delightedly, "You see? We did not need the fish."

Before the darkness fell, they gathered some fruit, and they lit a fire for comfort, and they lay down under their blankets and slept.

When the girl awoke in the morning, her father was gone. She pounded the last of the coffee beans with a flat stone, and fetched water to cook them, and squatted over the pot till it boiled. She looked at the bright flowers he had given her last night; they were drooping sadly now, but she did not want to throw them away. He had given them to her instead of saying something for which he could not find the words. They were meant to be a comfort to her, to tell her that this *pobru bichu* must not take on more importance than it was worth. She was aware that the initial excitement of the hunt, an excitement that she had once shared, had gone from him too, and that now only a searing determination remained, a willful stubbornness that seemed to have taken a crushing hold on him. When he returned, he was carrying a brace of pheasants he had shot with his bow, and as he tossed them down, she asked, not looking at him, "Did you find them?"

His laughter was strained, as though he were trying to bring back that excitement for her while knowing that it was impossible. He sat down beside her and said, "Do you know? It came to me that the jaguar would run for the nearest water when the fire came, and she would see that there was water where we were last night, and also over here where we are now. So, I walked along the bank of the river, a long way *there* . . . and a long way *there*. I found the tracks of antelope, and two small coatis, and some porcupine, and a tapir, and an ocelot, and many snakes, and some turtles, and a mouse deer, and two jaguars." He paused, relishing the tale he was telling. "One of them was *my* jaguar. She came from the burning forest, and only a little while ago she reached the river here and turned along the bank. She tried to catch a fish, but she was not able to do this. Then she ran after a trumpeter bird, which ran away from her. Can you believe it? She could not catch it. So she went back and ate the eggs, and now she is moving very slowly . . . that way, toward the mountains there. There is something wrong with her head now, perhaps from the fight with the dogs. When she lies down, her head does not keep still, but it jerks, this way and that. And on four legs she can walk only a little way, and then she uses three legs again, just as she did before. Also, she was burned in the fire."

The girl asked, her eyes wide, "How can you know all these things?" In spite of her sadness, she was amazed by her father's expertise.

He said, "It can all be read in the signs. She scratched herself against a thorn tree, and among the hairs there, some of them are burned." He was beginning to feel the pathos of the story he was telling, and he shook his head. "I do not think that she can last for much longer." The sadness in his own voice surprised him, and he was angry. He pushed the two birds over to her roughly and said, "Clean them; we will eat."

She went a little apart and began to pull off the feathers from the still-warm bodies, and slit them open with his knife and eviscerated them, and lit a fire to roast them on sticks; and all the time she said nothing. She glanced back once to see that her father was carefully selecting his best arrow, the one with the long iron tip that was not barbed, sighting down it for perfect straightness. He flexed his bow once or twice, and when he looked and caught her eye, he was angry because she looked so quickly away from him.

They ate the two pheasants in silence, and when he was ready to move off, he stood up and simply jerked his head at her instead of telling her to come with him.

A few paces behind, her eyes cast down, she followed him.

She was running now with a queer, lopsided gait. The wound at the back of her neck, the one she could not see, had damaged the spine, and her reflexes were slow. Her head would start twitching uncontrollably, and she would fall down, conscious but without command of her limbs. She would thrash around in the sand or the mud for a few moments, trying unsuccessfully to control the motion of her head. It would go of its own accord in a little while, and as the day went by, the attacks became fewer and further apart.

She could not reason about the resistance she was building up inside her, nor about the grasses she was eating to ease the pains; but slowly her strength was coming back.

She had eaten a clutch of eggs that a trumpeter bird had been sitting on. She had heard the strange resonant note that the plump bird kept calling from the depths of its stomach, and she had stalked it and then pounced from a few feet away. To her surprise, it had moved faster than she did, running quickly on its long green legs and waving its bright green bill around as it took to the air; she saw the broad red bands on the underside of its wings as it swooped low over her head and then found an unsteady perch in the branches, trumpeting noisily. She was not aware of how slow her movements had become, how sporadic and uncertain. There were times when both her rear legs would twist around and drag, and she would pull herself along by her forelegs without really knowing what she was doing; there was only the will to survive until recovery came of itself. She made a halfhearted effort to climb the tree, but the bird flew off before she had left the ground, so she stumbled back and satisfied her appetite on the eggs that were in the nest on the ground, eight of them, as brilliantly green as the bird's long legs and bill.

They were insufficient to satisfy her raging hunger, and she lay on her belly by the river for a while, scooping at the fish she saw there; her movements were too slow and unco-ordinated to catch them, and she gave up and climbed an outcrop of rock to take her bearings.

She pulled herself heavily to the top and fell down on her side, panting hard; and when she was rested from the effort, she moved to the edge of the bluff and looked out across the rolling hills and the forest.

There, in the distance, not too far away, she could clearly see the mountains where she lived. There was the great dark stand of shady trees that told her that a little to one side there was a red slope of sandstone split in two with a purple slash of granite, where a huge banana tree, fallen in the rains, lay athwart the cave that was her home. The sight of it, so close now, seemed to strengthen her.

She lay down on her belly, her head erect, and looked over the green treetops; her head had ceased its twitching, and the caked blood had hardened over the dreadful wound in her neck. Under the blood the healing process had already begun.

She needed to rest. But more, she needed the comfort that the sight of her distant lair brought to her. Over there, in a short while now, she could lie down in the shade that

she had known all her life, with all the old familiar scents around her, and the sound, just so, of water, and the cool dampness that came with the night.

There everything would be all right again; it was her home.

Urubelava too was staring out at the mountains.

He had found a great mango tree, more than eighty feet tall, and had climbed up into its higher branches. From this height the tops of the surrounding trees were a lush carpet of a thousand different greens, spotted brilliantly here and there with purple orchids and yellow flowers and the carmine splashes of the wings of roosting birds. A flight of pink herons had taken over the canopy of an emerald-colored thorn tree; and the light up here, compared with the semi-darkness and constant shadows of the jungle below, was blinding.

But under the hot blue of the sky, where the soft-gray clouds drifted in little puffs, far away on the horizon, the land rose gently to a high peak, where the colors were in sharp contrast. The soil was red over there, porphyric red, with wide scars of blue granite running through it. There was a great field of wild mustard on a high raised patch of dry ground, and a little below it there was a huge stand of well-watered bananas.

The peak stood out sharply above the rest of the land, commanding it; it was like a beacon set above the forest and the jungle and the rolling, watered hills. And it was a long day's march away, but no more.

For a long time Urubelava sat there, thinking about the

peak. And he was wondering how he could bring the bright smile back to his daughter's face.

He peered down through the branches and saw her sitting at the base of the tree; and when he called to her, making a soft birdlike sound by tapping his hollowed cheek with his fingertips, she looked up quickly and smiled at him. He waved to her. Come up.

She tucked her robe tighter around her thin body and began to climb, and he stretched down a hand when she had almost reached him and took her wrist and yanked her up so that she could squat beside him on the broad branch.

He parted the branches for her, broke off a heavy twig that was in the way, and pointed to the far red peak, and said, speaking very slowly and watching her cunningly, "You see that red hill over there, where the blue rocks are? And the banana trees?"

She nodded, wondering what great delight he was going to show her.

He said, still watching her, "That is where the animal lives."

There was no change in her expression. She said, "There is so much of jungle that a man could walk through it all his life and never come to the end of it. And there are so many animals that he could never count them." She could not resist it: "More animals than there are para trees by the river."

"And that is still where this animal lives."

"How can you possibly know this?" She was not afraid to question his wisdom; she was sure, even, that he would not strike her for it.

He was watching her eyes, seeking out the change in her mood as he would seek out tracks on the ground, reading them carefully, thinking about them for a long time, and then making up his mind.

He said slowly, "I told you that the animal was moving, all the way from the place where we first saw the tracks, in a straight line. From that place by the river, where the crocodiles were, all the way to the red rocks there, everything that has happened to the *onca* has happened in one long line. This means that it is going always in the same direction, no? That direction leads to the hills there, and the hills there are jaguar country. I know this, because I am a hunter." He pointed over to the west. "There, where the big *eisura* trees are, there will be no jaguars, only birds and porcupines; no monkeys, even." He pointed to the west, "There, by the yellow bushes, there will be no animals at all." Another direction. "There, by the black rocks, there is only marsh, and there will be snakes, and peccaries, and tapirs, and perhaps a few coatis, and many birds; but no antelopes, no ocelots, no jaguars." He swung his arm back to the peak again and said firmly, "Jaguar country. This is where my jaguar lives, and this is where my jaguar is going. It is the truth."

She thought for a long time, winding and twisting a piece of her robe between her fingers. She said at last, "*We* are moving through the forest. But *we* are not going home."

"For the jaguar it is different." He said, "The jaguar is going home to die."

When she did not answer him, he was suddenly very sure of what had happened, of something that for so long now he had not wanted to believe. He was quite certain; the jaguar, an animal of no importance, had somehow contrived to insinuate itself between him and his daughter.

And there was nothing he could do about it. Could he

retreat from a position he had taken? Could he unmake a decision that had cost him so much effort?

He was thinking: *No, she must learn that when a thing is stated, it must be done. It is not good to turn away from a purpose because of a foolish child's idea; and this is what she must learn; this is what I must teach her.*

chapter fourteen

This was the crucial place and the crucial time.

For ten or fifteen miles the land sloped gently upward, with water trickling back the way they had come. The black volcanic soil, enriched for millions of years by the falling leaves of the forest, gave way to dry sand, and then to broken boulders; and then, at last, where the undersoil had produced an unexpected marsh, the black soil came again, but wetter now and treacherous to move upon. The soil changed to blacker water, interlaced with the tendrils of strange plants that sometimes opened up in the evening with white flowers that gave off a sweet and sickly smell.

And then, abruptly, the red sandstone was there, rising high above the marsh in a steep, precipitous slope that was split here and there with the purple granite. The cliff, like the marsh, was a barrier; but at its top there was another abrupt change in the scenery of this constantly changing land; it was friendlier here, and softer, and more satisfying to the eye. The jungle noises were muted, and there were cool breezes, and the colors were more gentle. There were wide rivers, and deep-gouged creeks, and small streams that twisted and turned among the trees; there were sweet-scented bushes, and brilliantly colored flowers; there were tall, slender trees, and dark-green canopies, and emerald ferns, and lacy, swaying vines; and there was always the soft whisper of the leaves.

And for Bichu, it was filled with familiarity.

She was moving slowly now, not forcing herself anymore, because home was in sight. She was prepared to suffer the pains as long as they should last. The wound in the back of her neck, from time to time, still troubled her deeply, but the awful twitching had stopped. The wounded foreleg was almost constantly usable again, and for a long time now the strong rear legs had functioned properly.

She had passed her crisis, and she knew it. Now it was merely a matter of waiting, of resting as much as possible, of slowly regaining the strength and resistance that had once been hers. True, there were difficult pieces of terrain that now she found impossible to traverse, but there was always a way around them. She had found herself unable to climb, once, over a barrier of dark-brown fallen tree trunks, where bees were swarming. But now it was all a question of time, and in her home there would be all the time she would need.

Her long body had slimmed down in these last few days. Her belly was constantly empty, and this was her biggest problem. She still could not hunt, and her fishing had proved a slow and wasteful effort. Once she had found a freshly killed bird that a hawk had left, flying off at her approach; and she had overcome her revulsion at eating carrion and had made an unsatisfying meal. But for the most part she had eaten only eggs and the medicinal grasses that her instinct told her to chew on; and her great weakness stemmed, in part, from the constant hunger. It is good fresh meat that brings strength; and the absence of it was painful and dangerous to her.

She moved on steadily, easing herself up the slope, over the shallow waters, padding over the black soil and slipping under and through the tangled bushes, constantly heading toward the marsh and the sandstone cliff that lay beyond it. The dangers were all behind her; all she needed now was patience. She knew she was no longer going to die now.

Urubelava had stopped to gather wild coffee beans. He did not need to do this, and they were not even satisfactory to use before they dried for a week or two in the sun. But he picked a few handfuls nonetheless, and piled hot embers over them to roast them, and refilled the little bag when they were ready; it was the scent of them he craved, as a man craves a drug.

It was open country here, gently rolling country that gave him long views toward the mountains.

As he crouched on his heels, dribbling the beans slowly into the bag, a movement caught his eye and he turned to stare. Abruptly he grabbed at his daughter and pulled her under cover, peering out through the bushes and looking for the movement that had startled him. And then he saw it.

A yellow-and-brown movement, a spotted, camouflaged movement that lasted only a second or two; but it was enough.

Far across the open space, where the green grasses turned to yellow and then to brown, he saw the animal, the *pobru bichu,* crossing the ridge where the wild hibiscus grew, the tiny, pendent flowers splashing the greens with blood-red spots.

And then she was gone.

His eyes were bright with excitement and triumph. The brief glimpse was justification for all his stubbornness, and he turned to look at his daughter, his face creased with eagerness. He grinned and said, "I told you. The *bichu* is over there; did you not see?"

He stared at the ridge, knowing there would be no more sight of her, not yet, because she had crossed over to the other slope. He was elated, and as the girl climbed slowly to her feet and stood beside him, he said, "There, where the red flowers are, on the other side of the hill." He did not take his eyes off the spot, fixing it in his mind, and said, "This is the end, daughter."

The ridge was high above them, three miles away or more; and only a forest Indian could have been so sure of his sight.

He said, "She was walking, not running, and she is looking for food, and now I will catch up with her."

His daughter did not answer him. One hand to her mouth, her eyes screwed up against the bright light, she was staring out at the ridge, sensing the pride and the triumph in her father's voice. She took a long, deep breath. His hand was on her arm. "Now, this is the end. If you cannot keep up with me, then follow." He pointed to the land beyond the ridge, the high hills, and said, "There, by the blue rocks. You see? That is where I will be if you lose me. Try to keep close to me, but if you cannot, go to the blue rocks, and I will be there. And it will all be finished."

He tucked his knife more securely in his belt, slung his bow and his arrows over his shoulder, flexed his injured foot once, and said again, "Try to keep up with me. If not, there, by the blue rocks." It was the first time he had ever contemplated leaving her alone; she was frightened.

He turned away and began to run.

It was not necessary to test the direction of the wind. It was so slight that even the pinnate leaves of the tamarind trees were not stirring. But for Urubelava it was enough; his scent was being carried back behind him.

He ran lightly, on the balls of his feet, with his heels never touching the ground, moving quite fast but conserving his energy for the final burst. As he ran, he searched the horizon for his easiest route, not to the ridge where the jaguar had so briefly shown herself, but to the hill beyond it, to the sandstone and the slashes of granite, where he was sure she was headed. There would be no more tracking, no more of the laborious reading of signs—not till he reached the mountain ahead of him and prepared himself and his weapons for the kill.

He was even certain where the kill would take place. He had seen the marsh and dismissed it as a barrier to him but not to the animal. He had seen, too, the red cliff. *And this,* he was thinking, *this is the place, when she climbs the cliff. . . .* It was merely a matter of getting there fast. In all his life Urubelava had never before been so certain of anything.

One hand was firm on his knife, holding it steady at his waist, and the other moved slightly with the rhythm of his legs. His barrel chest would show no laboring even if he should have to run like this for the whole of the day. He glanced up at the sun and thought, *It is good; there is much of the day left.* The animal was out of sight, above and beyond the ridge, and it was not yet necessary to keep to the cover of the trees and the bushes; that would come later. It was not even necessary to run in silence; that, too, would come in the final, killing stalk.

He did not look around. He could hear his daughter running behind him, keeping up with him easily; her lungs not yet feeling the strain. She ran more lightly than he did, but with more noise.

As though an alarm had been sounded, a flight of green and carmine parrots left their tree and flew off, squawking as he ran below them. The trunk of a fallen ironwood tree lay across his path, and he scrambled lightly, easily, over it and ran on, hearing the girl climbing it behind him and neither stopping to help her nor looking back at her; he heard her fall and get to her feet again.

A stand of araucaria pines, more than seventy feet high, made a wide canopy over his head as he ran over the fallen needles, always keeping the same steady pace. An antelope bolted off into the bushes. He made a slight detour to avoid an army of dark-red ants that were marching in column at an oblique angle to his path. He heard a margay spit at him from the low branch of an overhanging balsa, and he paid no attention to it. A patch of wet swamp was dark with a hovering cloud of mosquitoes, and he veered to one side and back again, never slackening the easy, rhythmic stride. He dropped quickly to his knees when he passed a clear stream and drank briefly, scooping up the water into his mouth and then running on again.

And his daughter kept up with him, all the way.

A steep rise now, the land sloping up to the yellow of the hilltop, where the bushes were squat and stunted, and then down again into wetter ground, with the sound of running water all around them. Out into the sunlight and back into the dark jungle shadows, and sunlight again and more forest; and open space and dried grasses, and tangled vines and wetly rotting tree trunks that had been thrown to the ground by the rains. A long, dark stretch of tunnel through the dense trees, so tightly matted that he was using his knife now as he ran, slashing quickly and dexterously at the inter-twined lianas and forcing a way through them with scarcely a check in his pace.

He heard the girl call out to him, and with a gesture of impatience he turned and ran back a few paces; she was caught in a long vine that had tangled itself around her body, and he grinned at her, pretending not to notice the tears that were making little rivulets down the grime on her face. A few quick slashes with the *facao* and he freed her, using the knife almost like a whip, tossing the fallen strands to one side. There were deep scratches on her arms, where the thorns had torn her smooth, shining brown skin, but he paid no heed to them at all. He turned back and began to run again, aware that she was following him once more; he was a little surprised that she had kept up so well. He was thinking to himself, *Soon she will fall back, and then it will be easier for me. . . .*

The jungle thinned out and became bush, and then a small patch of forest, and then dry grass. The ridge with the hibiscus was on his flank and behind him now, and the blue-granite rocks were ahead, high above him over the marsh, a target to aim at.

He plunged into the wet mud, hardly slackening his pace, the slimy, clinging mud up to his knees and then to his waist. It was hard going here, and he looked back and saw, with astonishment, that his daughter was still there, only a few yards behind him, splashing her way through, half wading, half swimming; she had moved a little to one side, where the mud was wetter, and it was splashing up over her body as she tried to swim through it, sinking down as the slime dragged at her, and forcing herself to its surface again. He knew the dangers of the sucking mud, and he was alarmed for her; a man could move across it only if he held himself upright and walked slowly, using his widespread arms as floats. She was struggling too violently; the wet quicksand under the mud was a fearful thing. He shouted to her angrily, "There is time; there is no hurry." She did not answer him.

There were leeches sucking at his blood already, and a million insects were clouding around his head; some of them were attacking his eyes, and he brushed at them furiously, blinking away the poison. His breath was coming faster now, and he was beginning to feel the strain.

But his young daughter was still close behind him.

The marsh came to an end at last, and he pulled himself onto dry ground and lay for a moment, panting. And then, not looking back, he crawled over to a clear pool and dropped into it, brushing away the myriad insects, tearing off the swollen leeches. In a little while she fell into the water beside him, and he reached over gently and began to pull the leeches off her legs as she rubbed at her hair to kill the angry little *pium* flies.

For a short time they stayed there, cleaning off the ticks and the fleas and the sucking insects, and he said at last, "Better you stay here and wait for me. Soon I will come back, and we will go to the river and count the trees together."

She could sense his uncertainty. Saying nothing, she shook her head. And when he got up and began to run again, she followed him. Ahead of them the steep red cliff, the cliff he had thought of as the killing place, was less than a couple of miles away.

The wind changed; and with it, all the smells of the land changed too.

The oleander was upwind, and the thyme downwind; when the breeze turned, the scent of one replaced the other. There were a thousand new smells—of ripe tobacco leaves, of basil, of rotting cherimoya, of fallen guava, of fresh water, of decaying humus, of sweet lemon and sour sapote; of water antelope and armadillo, of monkeys and alligators, of herons and snakes and fish.

And with them came the scent of her old enemy.

For a startled moment Bichu remembered the touch of the hands at her throat, the smell of the rope that had been around her neck; and then, in a reflex so fast there was no time even to think, she was streaking for cover.

There were few bushes here, and no dense thickets, but she found a cluster of round red boulders that were covered with trailing bouganvillea, dark green and bright purple against the sandstone; and she swung around on her haunches underneath it and looked out, her eyes sharp, her senses alert.

She saw him then, saw the two of them, running toward her with an easy, regulated stride, not more than a thousand yards or so away. She coughed once, a warning, though she knew it was useless, and her quick eyes covered the territory all around her and saw that it was bad; the rocks here were a trap. She looked up at the steep slope above her, knowing that her home was at the top, with good cover there, and a way out of danger, and then she was racing, moving faster than she had ever moved before, across the hard red rock and the patches of yellow weeds.

There was not enough cover, and running would disclose her position to the enemy, but her great speed had been her ultimate help before, and now . . . After all this time and all this distance, the stubborn enemy had found her. All that was left was the talent of her speed, to outrun him, once and for all. The pain and the injuries were nothing; all that mattered was the final lap to her lair at the top of the cliff.

She sped fast over the flat ground, a yellow-and-brown streak of lightning, so close to the earth she was almost part of it, her tail held back, her rear legs pumping, her forelegs reaching out and devouring the land.

Just like the gauchos, he yelled out, *"Onca!"*

It was a cry of victory. Not stopping the running he unslung his bow and his arrows; and then he doubled his speed as he began to race over the hot ground, his legs moving like pistons, his arms flailing now. The sweat was running down his chest, and the perspiration from his forehead was dropping into his eyes and blinding him. His daughter shouted behind him, but he did not stop or slacken his pace. His breath was coming faster now. This was the moment for which he had conserved his energy; and now he was pushing it to its utmost.

Behind him, his daughter ran faster and stumbled, and fell and dropped back, and ran on again. This race was not for her, but somehow she must still keep up. Her body was torn with the pain of her bursting lungs, and it seemed that there wasn't enough air to satisfy them; but she too drove herself on with that splendid reserve of energy that only desperation can muster. He was getting ahead of her, fast; a hundred yards, two hundred, five hundred, running faster than she would have thought possible for anyone to move. Soon he was more than half a mile ahead, not slackening his speed. She could see the jaguar clearly, racing over flat red rock that gave no cover, heading for the broken mountain and gaining on him. It was a question, she knew, of endurance. Soon the pace of the animal would slacken, and the growing distance between them would begin to shrink. Then there would be another burst of speed, and once more it would grow. And then, again, the slowing down. And this would go on if necessary, for the rest of the day, until, at last, the man would still be running and the animal would be turning to fight, its muscles quivering, its chest pumping as it sought to gulp in more breath. And then . . .

She could not bear to think about it.

She was no longer crying. She felt she must keep running, that if she should fall now, or give up, all that she ever wanted in her life would be nothing. She could not explain her reasoning or even understand it, nor would she have been able to articulate it; but the instinct was in her too. And so, erratically and only barely conscious, she continued to run, to try desperately to keep up, passing the limits of endurance and still struggling.

Urubelava came at last to the cliff, and there was only silence. Even the birds were stilled.

His mouth was wide open, to take in fresh air without the sound of heavy breathing. The strain had been great, even for him. He was wet with perspiration, and the movement of his chest was heavy and rhythmic. He held his bow in his left hand, his best arrow in his right, ready to set the notch to the string, and he was looking around him in puzzlement.

The jaguar was gone.

Fifty paces ahead of him, less than that, the red cliff reared up steeply, broken here and there with gullies in which muddy streams were pouring down. A narrow white waterfall gushed from the top and fell to the bottom with a pleasant, refreshing sound, washing the rocks below, the residue spilling out into a rivulet that turned back and disappeared underground at the base of the cliff. Some vines were hanging, swaying gently. An upended tree was wedged along the slope, its roots in the air and its branches pointing downward. Some scarlet flowers were sending their probing roots into the soil, like fingers searching toward the water. There were broken ledges like old paths, some wide, some narrow, some opening out into small caves. A cluster of ferns told of a small pool halfway up the slope. The blue sky was hot and still, and the silence was broken only by the padding of running footsteps behind him. He turned around to make a signal for silence.

He was shocked when he saw his daughter. Her eyes were wide, and she was gasping for air, and her arms and legs were moving like broken limbs as she twisted around and collapsed to the ground, falling on her back and lying still. He put aside his obsession and ran to her, dropped on one knee beside her, and put a hand on her shoulder, his eyes uncomprehending, knowing only that she had driven herself beyond her capability and was at the point of collapse.

He whispered, "Why? I told you, there is time. . . ."

She shook her head numbly and rolled over onto her stomach and got onto all fours. She stayed there for a while, her head drooping between her upper arms, and then she rolled over and fell again. He did not know what he should do, and he touched her shoulder again, trying to comfort her and not knowing how to; and then she got heavily to her feet and stood there swaying, and she said thickly, "It is all right. I am all right."

She sank to her knees then and swayed gently from side to side, with her hands at the side of her face, the fingers just delicately touching the cheekbones.

He hesitated, and at the precise moment that he turned back to watch the rocks for a sign of the animal, a small shower of pebbles came dribbling down the side of the hill. He raised his eyes.

The jaguar was there, in full sight, not more than fifty feet above him. She was crawling along a narrow ledge on the face of the cliff, a narrow, upward-sloping ledge that was steep and scarcely wide enough for her body. He saw that she was moving painfully, dragging herself toward the cover of the hanging vines, and as he watched, the animal looked down and stared at him. She turned away almost at once and moved slowly into the vines and out of them again, moving toward the top of the cliff. The ledge was dwindling to nothing, and she was clinging to the sandstone like a butterfly pinned to a board. Now she was sixty paces away.

Urubelava slipped his favorite arrow onto the string, notching it carefully, testing the tension of the bow. The shaft was still dead straight as he sighted down it, sighted at a dark-brown scar on the back of the jaguar's neck, just over the spine. The neck shot, he would have called it, the instantly killing shot. The animal was moving quite slowly, moving toward the flattop of the outcrop.

He pulled back on the string till it reached his cheek, letting it cut deeply into his flesh and holding it steady; he could feel the tension at his shoulder, the string biting into his fingertips, the strength of this bow, made with his own hands many years ago. The sun was shining on the iron arrowhead where he had sharpened it.

The scar on the animal's neck was quite clear now. It was an easy shot. And now was the time to loose the shaft.

He held the tension and twisted his head to look back

at his daughter; she had not moved. She still knelt on the ground, with her hands to her cheeks, and she was watching the jaguar over his shoulder. The huge black eyes flickered once to look at him, then back to the target. She did not speak; it seemed that she was not even breathing.

He turned back to check his sighting. A hundred paces now, a trifle less, a good clean shot. He held the tension, pulling back just a little on the string.

Urubelava took a long, deep breath. And then he lowered his bow slowly to the ground and released the tension on the string. He unnotched the shaft and held it loosely in his hand.

Behind him, he could hear her shudder, and then it was silent again. He looked up at the cliff, and the jaguar was gone. It would be over the top now, heading for home by the blue granite, by the red sandstone and green banana trees. He turned around and stared at his daughter. The long fingers had gone from the cheeks, and the hands were loose at her side now, upturned and just resting on the ground; her eyes were on him.

He said angrily, "It was my choice. You understand that? It was my decision."

When she did not answer, he came over to her. She put out a hand and touched his hip, and rested her face against his thigh, and he said, more gently now, "I could have killed the *bichu;* I could have killed it easily. I chose not to. You understand that? It was my own choice."

She looked up now at the cliff beyond him, narrowing her eyes to peer against the sun.

The jaguar was there. Bichu stood for a brief moment on the edge of the high bluff, looking down on them; she had escaped them at last. The long, beautiful body was outlined against the sky, the tail just moving slightly, the round head

twisted to one side the better to keep them under observation. For a moment or two she stayed there, poised against the blue sky on the edge of the bluff with the bright sun shining on her, the most lovely animal in the world; and then she was gone, limping into the cave that was her lair, her home; and the young girl knew that she would never see her again.

She climbed to her feet and held on to her father's arm, resting her head against his shoulder. He was surprised at the affection, and puzzled by it, though it pleased him very much.

He took her arm and said, "Come. We will go back to the river and count para trees. It is a long way away; there will be much walking to do."

As they moved off together, he looked down at her and away again, not knowing whether or not she wanted to talk.

He asked at last, "Are you hungry, daughter? I can shoot a bird, if you would like. Or we can catch some fish at the river. Or there is plenty of fruit on the other side of the marsh."

He remembered the pampas they would have to cross, and the stretch of burned-out forest, and the waterfall where he had been bitten by the snake. He looked back once, almost sadly, at where the jaguar had gone, and knew that he was leaving a dream for the world he shared with the daughter he loved so much.

He remembered his injured foot then and began to hobble, and she put an arm around his waist to help him.

There were just the two of them walking back to the river, just the two in a land so vast that a man could walk for all his life and see nothing but the trees, and the rivers, and the mountains, and all the beauties of the splendid jungle.

About the Author

Alan Caillou is an author with a thirst
for adventure. During World War II he served
with the British Intelligence Corps behind
enemy lines in North Africa, was captured
by the Italians, and escaped just before
his scheduled execution. He then joined
the guerrillas to fight in Yugoslavia and Italy.
After the War, he returned to Africa to become
a safari guide. At present, Mr. Caillou makes
his home in California, where he divides
his time between writing and acting.

OLD YELLER

"We called him Old Yeller. The name had a sort of double meaning. One part meant that his short hair was a dingy yellow, a colour that we called 'yeller' in those days. The other meant that when he opened his head, the sound he let out came closer to being a yell than a bark."

The big, ugly, yellow dog loomed up out of nowhere one night and stole his way into the hearts of the warm family who lived in Birdsong Creek. And by his courage and daring, his duty and devotion he soon won his way into the hearts of everyone who came near him.

"Handled with the vividness and vibrant description of a new Hemingway."   SHE

"These hardy folk with their rough dog in an untamed country simply become life while you are with them."
                    THE TIMES LITERARY SUPPLEMENT

THE INCREDIBLE JOURNEY

The Story of three animals who walked home

There was Luath, a young and gentle Labrador, with a red-gold coat and a noble head.

There was Tao, the hunter, sleek wheat-coloured Siamese cat.

There was Bodger, the old half-blind tough Bull Terrier, with a strong sense of humour.

Three animals who walked and ran, and fought and struggled together; who escaped death at almost every step; and who finally came home as though they could never again be parted from the dream of their incredible journey.

Two World-famous Animal Stories